I0788000

CRAIG HALLORAN

Dragon Wars: Ride the Sky - Book 18

By Craig Halloran

★ ★ ★ ★ ★

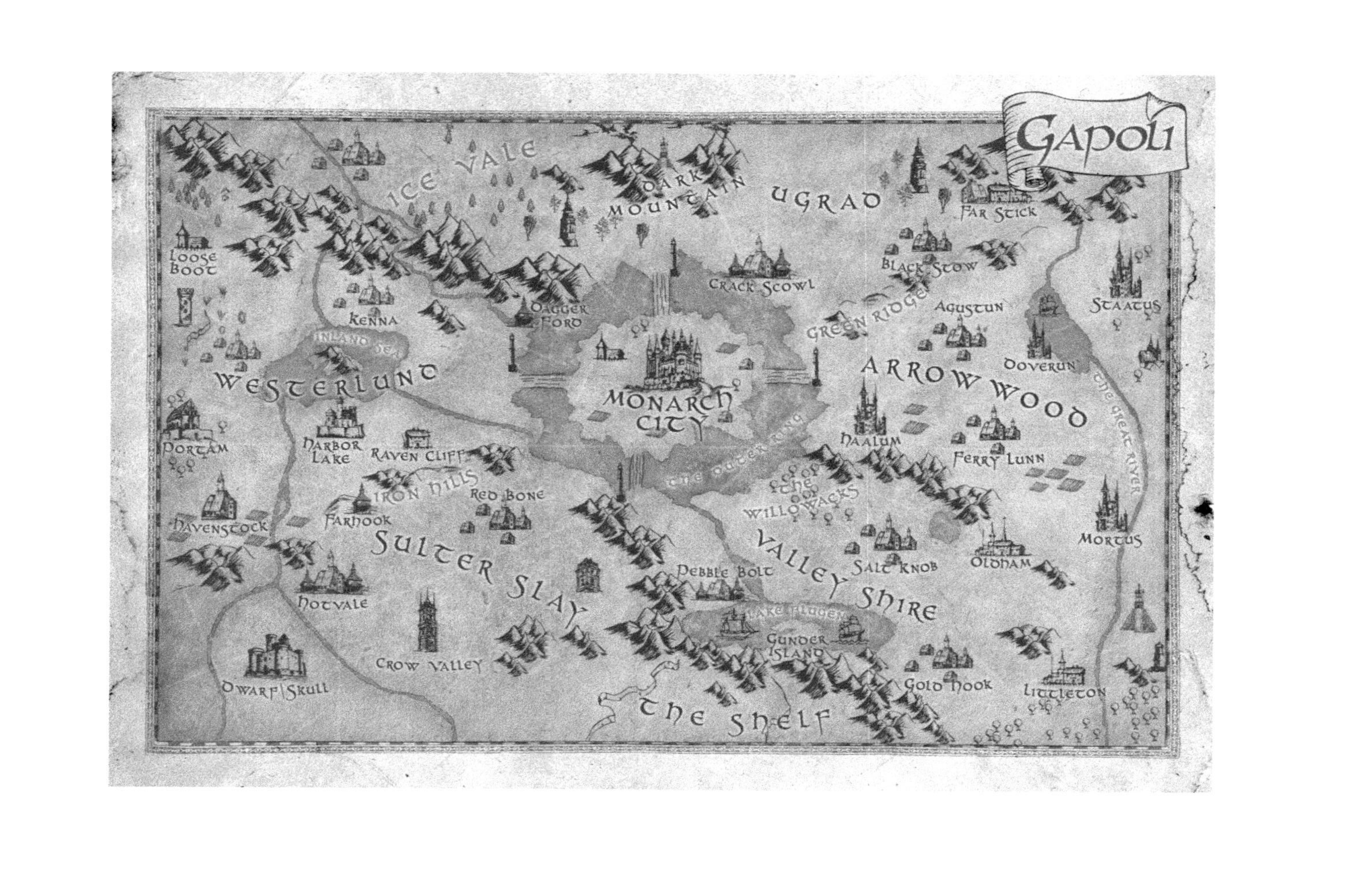

Gapoli
ICE VALE
DARK MOUNTAIN
UGRAD
FAR STICK
LOOSE BOOT
CRACK SCOWL
BLACK STOW
STAATUS
KENNA
DAGGER FORD
GREEN RIDGE
AGUSTUN
DOVERUN
WESTERLUND
INLAND SEA
ARROW WOOD
MONARCH CITY
PORTAM
HARBOR LAKE
RAVEN CLIFF
HAALUM
FERRY LUNN
The Outer Ring
The Great River
IRON HILLS
RED BONE
THE WILLOWACKS
HAVENSTOCK
FARHOOK
SALT KNOB
OLDHAM
MORTUS
SULTER SLAY
PEBBLE BOLT
VALLEY SHIRE
HOTVALE
LAKE PLUGEN
CROW VALLEY
GUNDER ISLAND
GOLD HOOK
LITTLETON
DWARF SKULL
THE SHELF

1

ARROWWOOD: DOVERUN

A PAIR of Golden Sentries carried Bowbreaker down the stairs that led to the dungeons. Their polished plate-mail armor was trimmed in gold plating. It covered the elven men from their necks to their toes. Spots of Bowbreaker's blood were smeared on it.

Through swollen eyes, Bowbreaker watched the stalwart soldiers' every move. They had him bound in chains and shackled at the ankles and wrists, and a collar pinched his neck.

They tossed him into a dungeon cell, fastened his shackles to the back wall, and locked them using a set of iron pliers.

After a long trial on a whipping post, Bowbreaker's aching body was drained. He sagged down the wall to the floor, licking his cracked lips. In a hoarse voice, he said to the soldiers, "You are the wrong side. You serve evil."

The elves didn't give him a parting glance. Their armor rattled softly, then the men were gone.

Bowbreaker scanned his surroundings. A broken cot half-covered in rotting hay lay nearby. A rat scurried across his cell, stopped in the middle, and looked at him while its whiskers twitched. His stomach rumbled. The rat scurried away, vanishing into a hole in the rock wall on the other side.

Stripped down to nothing but his trousers, Bowbreaker moved, the links of chain scraping over the floor. He winced the moment his raw back touched the wall.

He'd taken a beating—deservedly so, because he'd been caught. He'd abandoned Talon to resume his quest to kill Queen Esmarelda, a servant of Black Frost and a mistress of evil. She'd deceived his people. He was supposed to be their king. Yet he lived.

Chin up, he said, "So long as I breathe, my quest shall be fulfilled." He set his eyes on the doorway.

It had been five hundred years since his ancestors slew the last queen of evil that poisoned the elven land of Arrowwood. An arrow through the heart by one brave elf put an end to it. Good rose, and the green lands flourished, but not all the darkness was quenched. Over time, it festered, grew, and began to slowly spread its poison across the land. Once more, the beast rose to power, and that beast took the form of Esmarelda, Bowbreaker's former betrothed. Or so she thought.

Bowbreaker mulled over the actions that had led to his capture. After his attempt to take out Esmarelda the first time failed, he, Zora, and Crane managed a bold escape. He was supposed to journey with his friends to the Flaming Fence, but he thought of another opportunity to take out Esmarelda. She wouldn't be expecting him to make another attempt after the first failed one. He'd been wrong.

On the banks of the Great River, Bowbreaker watched a hurt Zora walk away. He knew the team could use him, but he had to fulfill his destiny. With his heart yearning to be with his comrades, he resumed his quest alone.

He slipped through the elven woodland like a ghost, avoiding all enemy troops that Queen Esmarelda sent after him. By the time he returned to the outskirts of Doverun, the patrols in the streets had been doubled. The ranks at the queen's castle had tripled. He maneuvered through the streets in a dusty cloak, disguised as a farmer. He hunched over, leading a cart of manure. No soldiers disturbed the fly-infested pile of animal excrement. Everyone let him pass.

Yet Bowbreaker hesitated. With the soldiers tripled around the palace, Esmarelda wasn't taking any chances.

She must have suspected that Bowbreaker might come back or, if not him, perhaps someone else. He moved his cart into the stables and considered departing.

Using the alleys, he navigated the backstreets. He climbed to the top of a tavern, which offered him a better view of the palace, hid, and waited for night to fall.

The guards on the palace walls changed out between dusk and dawn. They marched behind the battlements, passing one another from one side to the other. The palace windows were closed, and the balconies, empty of conversation. Bowbreaker saw no sign of Esmarelda or her attendants. They were sealed inside like a drum.

He managed a subtle smile. *Big mistake, Esmarelda. Now I know you're in there.*

He carried an elven hunting knife on his hip that was anything but ordinary yet easy to conceal. The curvature of the handle fit his large hand perfectly. Like his bow, it had been passed down to him, from generation to generation.

By bow or by blade, whatever it takes.

Night fell over the vast city that overlooked the docks of the Great River. The night was a cloudless night, and the moon shone like the brightest star, casting the darkest shadows in the corners and alleys of the black streets.

Bowbreaker abandoned his hiding spot. He climbed down the walls, jumped to the street, then landed as softly as a cat and headed toward Queen Esmarelda's palace.

He'd been there many times before and knew it like the back of his hand.

The first obstacle was bypassing the soldiers posted on the outer wall, which stood over twenty feet high. They were spaced out with several battlements between them, overlooking the street. More soldiers marched along the wall behind them.

From his hidden position across the street, Bowbreaker crouched and waited to make his move.

In the exterior wall were grooves broader than a man's shoulders, giving it an elegant design. But shadows covered them like black pipes.

He eyed the elves on the walls, waiting for them to look away from his direction, yawn, or even blink.

Bowbreaker's eyes darted from side to side. He zeroed in on their faces.

Then the call of a dragon sounded. *Skreee!*

The soldiers glanced up.

Bowbreaker scuttled like a rat to the break in between the walls.

2

BOWBREAKER SANK into the palace wall's seam and remained still. He heard another dragon call and waited. The outside conditions weren't as ideal as he'd hoped. Rain or a foggy night would have been better. No one liked the rain. It created a disturbance and favored the enemy by obscuring vision.

He exhaled, braced his feet and hands against the inner seam of the wall, and began to climb up the groove.

The clomping of horse hooves caught his attention. A patrol of four night soldiers approached the palace gate from the west, on a path to pass by Bowbreaker. He froze inside the gap and narrowed his eyes.

A horse and its rider walked by his position. The elven soldier sat tall in their saddle with their shoulders back, head turning from side to side as they scanned the road ahead. Their eyes grazed over the palace walls.

Another elven soldier looked right over Bowbreaker's position for what felt like a lifetime before the soldier turned his head aside and talked with another one. A few moments later, they passed through the entrance to the palace, and the gates closed them inside.

Ancestors be praised.

Bowbreaker resumed his climb. His strong hands and feet propelled him toward the top, where he waited beneath the battlements. He closed his eyes and listened. Elven soldiers were as stalwart as they came. The disciplined warriors were trained to hold their position for hours while moving little more than an eyelash. They could stare down a statue on a cold day rich with falling snow. Their senses were keen, making them observant as well as difficult to distract.

But a dragon call rattled nearly everyone, especially in the dead of night, after long hours of standing.

From the blackness in the sky, another call came like a lightning strike. *Skreee!*

Bowbreaker gambled. He stretched out his arm, hooked his fingers on a small niche in the wall, and swung himself over to the barefaced structure. Then he pulled himself to the top ledge and slunk between the battlements, crouching in the shadows.

The dragon call faded into the night.

He peeked around the battlements. The soldiers on the march moved in opposite directions. The ones standing watch faced the gap between the battlements and were looking outward. Quickly, Bowbreaker examined the palace windows and balconies. He didn't see a soul. After gathering his feet underneath him, he leaped from the battlement, cleared the walk, and dropped twenty feet down to a soft bed of grass on the other side.

Bowbreaker pressed his back to the wall and waited. Not another person was in sight. No sound of an alarm came. No foot soldiers patrolled the interior wall.

I made it.

He navigated through the gardens at a slow pace, keeping in the shadows of the shrubbery and trees. Voices inside the palace entrance carried outside. He smelled bread baking.

A host of dignitaries stepped outside one of the entrances. They smoked from curled pipes made of oxen horn. Yellow smoke built up and lingered above their heads as they moved onto the walkways that led through the gardens.

The dignitaries—military men carrying swords and wearing priceless ceremonial armor—passed by and moved on to another quadrant of the spacious courtyard.

A white-faced barn owl in the branches above Bowbreaker's head let out a shriek. He met its eyes and stuck out his arm.

The small owl dropped from its perch and landed on his wrist. Its talons dug into his skin.

Bowbreaker whispered, "You have a strong grip, little one." He stroked its feathers. "Perhaps you can be of service to me. I could use an ally."

The owl blinked its large chestnut eyes.

"Cooperation. I like it." It had been a long time since Bowbreaker spent time among the animals. He considered them all kindred spirits, and they had a strong connection. He covered the owl's face with his hand. "This won't hurt a bit. Let your eyes be my eyes."

Bowbreaker's eyes rolled up in his head. The owl fluttered. He felt a tiny heartbeat inside his body, and they became one. He removed his hand from the owl's face. His view of his surroundings sharpened, and a colorful sun ring formed around them.

"Inside the palace," he whispered. "I'm looking for someone. Find them. Quickly."

The owl spread its wings and took off into the night. It circled around the palace spires, soaking in everything it surveyed with crystal-clear vision.

Bowbreaker marveled at the keenness of the owl's vision. It saw the night as if it were day and spotted rats scurrying across the streets as if they were cattle at a crossing. It circled the tallest spire one more time, dropped down from the sky, and entered the palace.

Birds being inside the palace was common. They

nested in the vaulted ceilings and often left bird droppings. The servants had the task of rooting them out, but in the end, like with most castles, the birds won out. No one would be suspicious of an owl passing through, and it wasn't uncommon for their night shrieks to wake the occupants inside the castle from time to time.

Servants and dignitaries strolling the grand hallways paid the sailing bird little mind. All the people Bowbreaker surveyed were consumed in their own works and conversations.

He saw no sign of Queen Esmarelda, but his vision led him to the throne room, where many men and women of the races had gathered. Over a dozen dignitaries looked down on a great table. At the far end, Queen Esmarelda talked as she pointed at the figurines of soldiers scattered on a map of Gapoli. Tiny carved-out models of war ships were spread out along the Great River.

It took Bowbreaker but a moment to decipher what was going on. Queen Esmarelda wasn't defending her palace against him.

She's not worried about me. She's preparing to invade the East River elves.

He took a longer look at the figures on the map. Her forces were too numerous to count.

And with an army that size, she'll wipe out what is left of them.

3

THE DELEGATION of dignitaries in the throne room departed during the wee hours. Queen Esmarelda's soldiers escorted her to her bedroom in the higher levels of the palace. A pair of Golden Sentries carrying spears remained posted outside her door.

Perfect.

Bowbreaker broke his connection with the barn owl and rubbed his eyes, blinking away the colorful spots. Once his vision cleared, he devised a plan.

Soldiers were stationed throughout the castle's interior hallways, making it impossible to pass without being noticed—unless you were one of them.

A group of dignitaries remained outside in the courtyards, having a quiet conversation.

He cupped his ear.

One of them, an elf, spoke softly yet distinctly. "Look at all the extremes the queen is going to. There are soldiers everywhere. Does she think one of us would dare strike her down? How distrustful can she be?"

"Fool," an elven woman said. "Did you not hear that an assassin tried to take her life recently? An entire tower crashed into the streets."

"I heard a drunken dragon rider crashed into it," another man said. "What I wouldn't do to ride a dragon, but those Riskers terrify me."

"Don't be a dumb scutty," the first man said. "Who would believe such a tale?"

"The queen's men said it was a training accident."

The elven woman replied, "Don't believe everything you hear. The East River elves know she is going to pounce. They've sent assassins to take her out. That is what all this is about. It's best we mind our tongues for our own sakes. The last thing we need is to catch the ear of a queen's accuser."

"Agreed," the soft-spoken man said. "Let us depart with haste so that we don't cross an assassin's path." He laughed lightly and stepped aside on the path. "After you, milady."

The small delegation departed.

Huh. She isn't looking for me but rather a new enemy she's created. It appears my people in the east are still with me.

Bowbreaker stole his way across the courtyard and moved along the base of the palace walls. When he was young, he and Esmarelda had played games together. One of them was hiding in the castle. The servants had a network of passages behind the palace's interior wall, allowing them to travel unseen without disturbing the monarchs.

He found a back door that led to one of the kitchens. He slipped into the passage, down a small set of stairs, and into the kitchen.

A pair of elven women were scrubbing pots and pans. A heavyset elven man wore a white vest and black shirt, smoked a tobacco pipe, and rubbed down silverware with a cloth. All parties had their backs turned to one another. Bowbreaker moved between them into the next room.

He stood in the galley where the servants ate. The farm tables and benches had been wiped down. Not another person was in sight. The scuffle of footsteps caught his ear. He dropped to the floor.

A Golden Sentry entered the galley then moved halfway across the room and stopped.

Bowbreaker observed the man's feet turning his way and heard the knocking of metal knuckles on the table.

The portly elf in the vest hurried into the galley. "Commander Christo, how can I be of service?"

"It's been a long day," the commander said in a rich voice. "I could use some rations for my retainers."

"Oh, right away. Forgive me. I expected you earlier. I have bread set aside. I'll fetch it right away."

"No hurry. The days are always long, and I don't see that changing." Commander Christo sat down, slipped his gauntlets off, then put them on the table and sighed.

Bowbreaker sat up and peeked over the table.

Commander Christo sat with his back to him, rubbing his neck underneath his long graying hair. He cracked his neck from side to side. "I'm getting too old for this." He started to turn in his seat.

Bowbreaker lay back down. He didn't know Commander Christo, but a soldier couldn't rise to commander in the Golden Sentries without having some grit about him. He would be an easier mark than the younger ones, but no doubt he would have well-honed senses.

The elven kitchen manager returned with a large basket full of bread and set it on the table.

"I'll have my men return the basket in the morning. Thank you," Commander Christo said.

"Will you be needing anything else?" the kitchen manager asked.

"No. I'm heading to the armory to peel this suit off. Then I'll soak my aching toes and prepare for bed."

"Very well." The kitchen manager departed.

Commander Christo grunted as he stood. He dropped his gauntlets into the basket and headed toward the armory in the lower levels.

Bowbreaker trailed behind him.

4

THE ARMORY SERVED MULTIPLE PURPOSES. Complete with weapons racks and armor, it hosted bathhouses and tiled pools as well. Underground springs ran beneath the palace, offering warm water for the elite soldiers to soak in.

Commander Christo was the lone soldier in the facility. He sat on a bench, stripping off his armor piece by piece, while Bowbreaker kept himself concealed in a nearby storeroom. At first, Bowbreaker had thought he would need to take out the elven commander, but he could take a suit from the armory.

Once Christo peeled off his armor, he grabbed a robe from a peg on the wall, put it on, and headed into the steam of the adjacent pool room.

Bowbreaker stole a look as the elven commander sank

into the water. The mist obscured his view of the man, but he saw the elder elf close his eyes, lean back, and relax.

He waited. The commander didn't move.

Elves were notorious for long soaks in their baths and short swims from side to side.

He's old. He'll be a while.

Bowbreaker moved deeper into the armory, out of sight of the pool. He spotted a Golden Sentry suit of armor and started to put it on. Unlike most armor, the elven craft was lighter. It was designed to be quickly donned or shed. He dropped the breast plate over his shoulders and fastened the side straps without making so much as a sound.

The bracers, arms guards, and thigh and shin guards buckled into place.

Within moments, Bowbreaker was in a full suit of polished-metal armor. It fit snugly but was flexible enough. He buckled on a sword belt and grabbed a helmet.

"Pardon me," someone said. "And don't make any sudden moves. I'll skewer you."

Clutching the helm, Bowbreaker turned and faced Christo. The elven commander's hair was dripping wet and hung to the shoulders of his robe. Sword in hand, he kept his narrowed eyes on Bowbreaker as a puddle of pool water dripped on the floor beneath him.

"Keep those hands on the helmet," Christo said. "Though I'm certain that suit of armor is not yours." He sucked his teeth. "I thought I sensed a presence in the galley. Thought I didn't notice, didn't you?"

"I hoped."

"Don't let the gray hair fool you. I'm as keen as ever." Christo gave him a hard look. "Who are you? An assassin sent from the East River elves? A spy, perhaps?"

"Neither, though they are my brethren and your brethren as well." Bowbreaker looked deep into the elf's face. Christo's elegant features were hardened by time and battle. His gaze was as strong as hammered metal, but he spoke with the poise of a diplomat. "I am Bowbreaker."

Christo's eyes flickered. "I'll be. They said you were large for an elf. I should have known when you put Jumaan's armor on. He's one of the largest elves I've ever seen, but you're a speck bigger." He licked his teeth. "So, come to kill the queen, eh?"

"My destiny must be fulfilled. You would be wise to step out of the way."

"You know that's impossible. I am a Golden Sentry. My life belongs to the queen."

Bowbreaker's blood stirred. "She is a servant of evil who kills and enslaves her own people."

Christo shrugged. "Regardless, I gave my oath. It is not my place to challenge the anointed."

Bowbreaker clenched his jaw. The elven sense of duty blinded reason. He'd argued against it countless times but had given up long ago. "Where do we stand, Commander Christo?"

"You can make it simple and surrender, or I'll be forced to kill you." Christo glanced at Bowbreaker's hands, which were fastened on the helmet. "I have you at a severe disadvantage. I'd recommend that you don't try anything foolish. I'd hate to be the elf that split your skull open. A part of me admires you, in a strange sort of way."

"And I also admire you, Commander." Bowbreaker had nowhere to move. Inside the dressing closet, his back was almost to the wall. With one quick step, Christo would certainly run him through. He exhaled through his nostrils. "It's a shame that we don't see eye to eye."

"A shame, indeed, for you."

"Where to now?"

"Do you surrender?"

Bowbreaker ground his teeth.

"Heh. You aren't going to surrender, are you?" The wrinkles between Christo's eyes deepened. He thrust as quickly as a jumping cat.

Bowbreaker caught the tip of the sword inside the bowl of the helm. The sharp tip pierced through the metal and plunged toward his chest. He twisted the helm hand over hand, screwing the sword handle out of Christo's grip.

"Clever!" the commander exclaimed. "And quick!" He pounced on Bowbreaker.

Bowbreaker's right fist hit the elven commander's jaw with the force of a kicking mule.

The light in Christo's eyes went out before he hit the floor. He lay on the stones, as limp as a noodle and sprawled out like a rag doll.

Dragging the elder inside the dressing closet, Bowbreaker said, "You're not as fast as you think you are, Commander."

He closed the man inside and removed the sword from the helmet. Then he placed the helmet over his head and abandoned the armory.

Inside the main hallway, the soldiers saluted as he passed. With haste, he took the stairs and followed the hallway down to Queen Esmarelda's room.

Two Golden Sentries lowered their spears and stepped forward.

In an urgent voice, Bowbreaker said, "We have an intruder in the palace. I've come to alert the queen."

5

The Golden Sentries exchanged wary glances.

"What are you waiting for?" Bowbreaker asked with a demanding tone. "Alert the queen. Trouble is in our midst."

One of the golden sentries pulled back his spear and stepped backward then knocked lightly on the door.

A moment passed, and the door cracked open. One of Queen Esmarelda's handmaidens poked her head out. "Who disturbs the queen at this hour? She is weary."

"We have word of an intruder on the premises," one of the soldiers said. "Please notify the queen immediately."

The handmaiden's eyebrows rose. Her eyes grazed over Bowbreaker, and she vanished inside, closing the door behind her.

Bowbreaker stood as upright as a statue, keeping his

hands at his sides. He didn't say a word or even look at the soldiers, though he felt their uneasy looks on him.

Finally, the one that had knocked the door broke the silence. "What sort of intruder are we dealing with?"

"The kind that cut open the neck of one of our brethren."

The soldiers' eyes grew.

"Who?" the same elf asked.

"Commander Christo." Bowbreaker wiped his eyes with his thumb and finger. Lying didn't come easily, but at that point, it didn't matter. He only needed to get close enough to Esmarelda to finish her off. If he died, he died, but his people would be liberated. "Knock again. We can't afford to risk the queen's life."

The door swung open, and the handmaiden stepped outside. She looked at Bowbreaker and said, "You, enter and tell the queen your news."

Bowbreaker nodded and marched into the queen's extravagant quarters.

Queen Esmarelda stood in front of a vanity, tying the belt of a white silk robe that fit her perfect figure like a glove. Her lustrous blond hair hung down to the middle of her back, and she flipped one side over her shoulder. Aside from the handmaiden, she was alone.

The handmaiden closed them inside.

The queen ran a brush through her hair, and without turning, she said, "Tell me about this intruder, my loyal servant. Man, elf, orc, monster, dragon? Am I in peril? Or have my Golden Sentries dispatched him by now?"

Bowbreaker's hand slipped down to his sword handle. He didn't want to speak. She would know his voice. He scraped his sword out of his sheath.

The handmaiden gasped.

Queen Esmarelda turned, an amused smile on her beautiful face. Her captivating eyes met his. "My dear, sweet Bowbreaker. What a surprise. So, I take it you are the intruder sent here to kill me."

A chill swept over him. "You knew? How?"

"I saw your face through the peephole in the door. I have to admit your plan was a sound one. I did not expect you at all. But then I looked, and there you were." She stepped closer. "My strong and handsome betrothed. Relentless. I like it."

The handmaiden moved toward the door.

"Stay," Esmarelda said. "This matter is between Bowbreaker and me. I think it's time we settled it once and for all." She approached him.

He stuck the point of his sword out. "Don't come a step closer."

She gave a gentle laugh. "Why not? You want to strike me down, don't you?" She moved until her chest touched the tip of his sword. "Strike, Bowbreaker. Cut me down in cold blood. That's what you want, isn't it?"

The handmaiden fell to her knees and pleaded, "No, my queen!"

Esmarelda raised a finger. "Silence." Her magnetic eyes drew him in. "What are you waiting for, my betrothed? Slay me and fulfill your destiny. Plunge your weapon through my chest, and you can be the king who slew the defenseless queen. What's the matter, my love? Can't you do it? Are you strong enough to kill me? You tried to shoot me with your little bow. Why can't you take me with a sword? Hmm... is it too difficult to do face-to-face?"

The pounding in his ears fell silent as the hot blood racing through his veins cooled. "It is." He lowered his blade. "I can't cut you down in cold blood. That would be wrong."

"Yes, it would." She exhaled. "Oh, Bowbreaker, if you could only see matters from my point of view and not from the angle of your archaic virtues. I am saving our kindred from certain calamity."

"You side with the serpents of evil."

"Who is to say?" She nodded at her handmaiden.

The handmaiden opened the door, and Golden Sentries surged into the room. One of them knocked Bowbreaker to his knees, while a second soldier disarmed him. They bound his arms behind his back, put a rope around his neck, and pulled back.

"Easy, men. I need a word with him." Esmarelda

kneeled in front of Bowbreaker, nose to nose, then hugged him. She whispered in his ear, "You're right, Bowbreaker. I am evil. I am possessed. And all the elves, east and west, will suffer for it." She kissed his cheek. "You should have killed me. You had the perfect chance. Your heart failed. Long live Black Frost." She kissed his other cheek and walked away.

Bowbreaker dunked a wooden ladle into a bucket of water and drank. The guards brought him a bowl of porridge as well. He ate all he could.

Rotting in a dank dungeon cell was one matter. Rotting in your thoughts of failure was another. He'd failed. Queen Esmarelda's certain death had been in his hands, and he turned aside his blade.

Why? How could I not do what my ancestors did?

Evil queens in the past had risen and fallen. They'd been slain by the hands of his own family. Yet when presented with the perfect opportunity, he couldn't do it.

Deep in his heart, he knew why. Killing Esmarelda in cold blood was wrong. In battle was another matter entirely. Still, he wrestled with it. By her own admission, she was determined to obliterate her own elven race—not only the East River elves but the ones in the west, which had defended her, as well.

How can my people be so blind? Why do they not take

action? Can't they see she is destroying our people?

He'd gone over the problem a hundred times, if not a thousand. Perhaps Black Frost's influence had stretched out to more people than he thought.

My people have abandoned themselves.

A pair of guards entered the dungeon, holding up an elven man by the arms. He wore a cotton shirt that hung down past his knees. His gray hair hung over his eyes. They shoved the man into a nearby cell. Metal banged on metal as they locked the man inside, then they left.

The older man wheezed.

"Do you require aid?" Bowbreaker asked. "You don't sound well."

Links of chain dragged across the floor. The other prisoner said, "You've done enough damage, Bowbreaker."

He dropped the ladle into the bucket, stretched as close to his door as his chains would allow, and asked, "Commander Christo?"

"Your memory is sharp. A shame your sword wasn't. You should have killed that witch." Commander Christo wheezed. "Why didn't you finish her?"

Bowbreaker swallowed. "I couldn't. Why are you here? You've committed no crime."

"Do you jest? I failed to apprehend you. What did you think would happen to me when an assassin almost killed the queen? Huh? Did you think they would pin a medal on me?" Commander Christo let out a ragged sigh. "They placed all the fault on me. Decades of spotless service, and I'm judged by a tribunal of fools, all of whom kiss the queen's behind." He spat. "They called me a traitor. Accused me of consorting with you. They discovered I had East River blood in my veins and prosecuted me as such. Heh. I was brought over to the west when I was ten years old. Selected to be a Golden Knight. Times were peaceful then. Who thought that would come to haunt me? It would have been best if you had killed me. Now, my honor has been stolen from me."

"Don't blame me, Christo. How did you not see this coming?"

Chains rattled.

"You're right," Christo answered. "I knew. Her heart is as black as coal. But I had my duty. And who are you to blame me? You did not swing the sword yourself."

Bowbreaker raised his chin and laughed. "Look at us, bickering like old hens. I suppose we both failed. I wonder what's in store for us now."

"We will be made an example of for all to see. The queen keeps wild creatures that tear men apart." Christo chuckled. "If we're fortunate, she might give us a bamboo shaft to fight them with."

"What sort of creatures?" Bowbreaker asked.

Christo coughed and said, "There are no words to describe them other than this: abominations. That's what they call them. Abominations from the abyss."

WIZARD WATCH

GREY CLOAK STOOD in front of the Time Mural, staring at the blank wall of stone. He touched the cool surface and stepped back in front of the archway. "You're telling me that Gossamer is trapped in Bish?"

Datris nodded. The young elf's smooth face was a mask of concentration as he meticulously put the Pedestal of Power, which held the gemstones, back together. "Gossamer understood the intricacies of this mystic contraption better than I. Thankfully, Tatiana and Dalsay are here to assist."

"How long is this going to take? And I'm getting hungry again," Georgio, a brawny warrior with wavy brown hair, said. He wore a black-billed cap, a vest over his long-sleeve shirt, trousers held up by a belt with a large black buckle, and boots. His size almost matched that of Dyphestive, who stood nearby, talking quietly to another monster of a man nearly eight feet tall. "Not to mention I needed to be somewhere with a special someone tonight."

Tatiana gave a frustrated look to the otherworlders and said, "I don't think you're going to miss your date."

"Ah, she's going to kill me. I missed the last date and the one before that." Georgio took off his hat and scratched his head. "It's always something when you're with the City Watch. Maybe Lefty will take care of it."

Grey Cloak moved across the room and walked up the dais steps to where the pewter thrones sat. Nath sat in the one on the right, slumped over to one side. His long, stringy hair—gray with streaks of bright red—hung over his eyes. He swiped it away as he inspected the tiny divots in the metal arm of the chair.

"I can smell them. After all of these years, I still know their stench," Nath said under his breath in a scratchy voice.

Grey Cloak sat down and asked, "Who are you talking about?"

"Verbard and Catten. Wicked men. They almost killed me once." Nath's nostrils flared. He raised his head and surveyed the room. "The more life changes, the more it remains the same."

"Agreed. I feel as if we're running in circles."

"You aren't. It all serves a greater purpose."

Grey Cloak and Talon had made a hasty departure from Safe Haven and headed to the Wizard Watch tower in the southeastern end of Gapoli, near Littleton and the mountains Grey Cloak, Dyphestive, and Streak had once called home.

Waiting outside were the children of Cinder. All of his brood kept watch for their enemies from the skies and on the ground. Members of Talon were with them, including Zora, Crane, Anya, Razor, Gorva, Beak, and Tinison. The only one missing was Zanna. She was the speaker of the Nether Realm's prisoner behind the Flaming Fence.

They needed Zanna Paydark back. In a strange twist of events, she'd offered herself to Utlas in exchange for Talon's freedom, leaving it to Grey Cloak to find a way to get her back. He saw only one course.

"If we don't have Zanna, we can't send her back in time. If we can't send her back in time, she can't warn us," Grey Cloak said as he rubbed the divots on the arm of his chair. "This is impossible."

"Be patient a little longer. Have faith in your friends and your mother too," Nath offered.

"Do you know something I don't?"

"I know a lot of things you don't."

Grey Cloak smirked. "In regard to our current situation?"

"Oh, well, no, but I believe where one plan dies, another one is born."

"And I believe the plan of going to your world is madness," Grey Cloak said.

"You want to destroy Black Frost, don't you?"

Grey Cloak nodded.

"Black Frost has his eyes and allies all over this world, but he cannot see into another. In that lies the best way to defeat him," Nath said.

"Why don't you return?"

"It would surely kill me. That's why I had to escape. My world is drained enough. I can feel my bones wither from within. I'd be dead by now, had I stayed."

"Well, we aren't going anywhere if they can't fix the Time Mural," Grey Cloak said with a sigh.

"We'll have it working," Tatiana assured him. She placed more gemstones into the bowl. "One way or the other, it will work. It has to."

Brak's belly groaned so loudly that it echoed through the room.

Dyphestive laughed. "And I thought I hungered. This man could eat a dragon! No offense Streak."

Streak was lying behind the thrones, at the foot of the platform and said, "None taken."

"You'd better feed us, or it's liable to turn ugly again," Georgio warned them. "We need come buttered biscuits, and we need them soon. The last thing we want is Brak rampaging." He looked at the bloodstains on the floor. "Trust me."

Georgio had already colorfully illustrated the events that unfolded when they were transported from Bish back to the Time Mural chambers. Brak was in a berserk stage. He slaughtered Commander Covis and all of his men. Honzur the Necromancer died as a result of it as well. It was hours before Brak's temper came back down, and he stumbled upon a wizard pantry, which he raided.

Dyphestive nudged Georgio. "Come on. We can find food on our own. If it's not inside, we'll find it on the outside. The dragons will have hunted some sort of beast. They eat all the time."

Brak nodded.

Georgio grinned. "Any beast is good by me. I'll eat the horns and hooves if I have to."

"Not if I eat them first," Dyphestive quipped.

They departed through the main entrance.

Grey Cloak leaned forward to object but said instead, "Don't go too far." He sat back. "All right, Nath, tell me about this apparatus you were talking about."

"Ruune," Nath said.

"What?"

"It's called the Apparatus of Ruune. And it's powered by stones like those." Nath pointed at the hunks of gems embedded in the archway. "We call them Thunderstones."

7

Grey Cloak leaned forward on his elbows, watching the sorcerers. "Go on," he said. "I'm listening. Tell me more about these stones. I take it you've used them before."

Nodding, Nath rubbed his scaly black arms. "Long ago, the Thunderstones were a source of aid."

"How long ago?"

Nath shrugged. "Ages."

Grey Cloak rolled his eyes. "I don't even want to know how long that is. Do you even know where they are?"

Nath cleared his throat. "Not exactly. In order to keep them safe, they have been hidden."

"And I take it you know where they're hidden?"

"I know where they were last hidden. Again, that was ages ago. The guardians have possibly moved them several times since. But I know where to start." Nath winked a golden eye at him. "I'm sure you'll find it."

"Or we find another way to stop Black Frost now. That's what I've been saying all along. We go to his temple and destroy his connection to your world."

Tatiana and the ghostly form of Dalsay looked up.

"That's a death sentence," she said. "It is precisely what Black Frost wants."

"Agreed," Datris added. "I've spent a long time with Black Frost. His fortress in Dark Mountain is amply prepared for your arrival. For any enemy's arrival. There is only one way in, and he and hundreds of dragons guard it."

Grey Cloak gave them all a serious look. "That's why we distract him. Besides, you'll have to return with Gossamer either way. Perhaps it will be best to strike then."

"We don't know how to destroy Black Frost's portal or close it. It takes a long time to master such things," Datris replied. "At the moment, it is imperative that Gossamer and I return to Black Frost's temple. I must replace Zanna Paydark's statue. She must resume my place as me and hope to slip by Black Frost's notice. If it fails, well, I'll be a hunk of rock forever."

"I know the consequences." The mere thought of being turned to stone gave Grey Cloak chill bumps. At the moment, his mother was still stone, and so was Dyphestive's father. He stood up. "Let's focus on getting Gossamer back." He walked down the steps. "Is there anything I can do to help?"

With an expression of concern, Tatiana said, "You can look for more gemstones on the floor. We still don't have all of them."

He nodded and peered at the floor. "Glad to help."

Zora took in a deep breath of fresh air and observed the twinkling stars. She'd never noticed the sky so much before. Everything in nature, she'd taken for granted. A small patch of purple crocus flowers lay in a bed at her feet. The crickets chirped. Birdsong filled the sky. She smiled.

Crane ambled over and squatted, his knees cracking. "What are you smiling about?"

"Do you have something against smiling?"

"Heavens, no," Crane said as he sat down on a crocus patch. "Ah, this ground feels good. No matter how soft I try to make my wagon seat, my back always hurts." He winked at her. "It's an age thing. You shouldn't have to worry about that for a long while." He took a drink from a wine jug. "Want some?"

"No, thank you."

He raised his eyebrows and glanced at the sky. "Beautiful, isn't it? Makes you wonder why people fight all the time when all of us can share such beauty."

"Not if you're in the Nether Realm." She shivered. "The sky was nothing but fire. And Zanna is trapped there. I can't stop thinking about it. It's miserable, being trapped in a place such as that. As vile as those people are, I pity them."

"They made an unwise choice long ago. Hence, they suffer the consequences." Crane yawned. "Try not to worry about it. Our friends in the tower will think of something, I'm certain."

"Assuming they come back out." Anya had crept up behind Zora and towered over her shoulders. Her chiseled features stood out in the moonlight, and her eyes were like brewing storms. "They've probably been whisked away to another time and place, leaving us stranded to face the coming slaughter."

Zora said, "Give it a rest. If we can't trust each other by now, we never will."

"I don't think I'll ever trust a wizard. Not wholly." She eyed Crane's jug.

He flung the jug to her.

Anya drank deeply while eyeing the open entrance to the Wizard Watch. Dyphestive came out with two hulking strangers. She dropped the jug and pulled her sword in one fluid motion.

Zora sat up, eyes widening.

Crane turned his head over his shoulder and gasped. "Who is that monster?"

Zora had no idea. She hadn't been in the tower and didn't have any idea what was going on. She stood.

Dyphestive approached with an easy smile on his face. "These are Georgio and Brak. They aren't from Gapoli, but they're here to help us."

"Who are these gorgeous women?" Georgio asked. He took off his cap and bowed. "I am captivated."

"Indeed," Brak said in a deep voice as he took a knee. He was still taller than Zora. He grabbed her hand in his massive paw and kissed it. "What is your name, princess?'

Her words were caught in her throat, but she said finally, "Zora."

"A pleasure to meet you, Zora. Brak, at your service."

Razor stepped into the crowd, his hands on his sword pommels. "Not so fast, fellas. These women are with me."

8

———

BRAK ROSE to his full height and glowered down at Razor.

"They grow the trees big around here," Razor said. "But you know what they say. The bigger they are—"

"Will you ease up?" Gorva grabbed Razor by the back of the pants and pulled him away from Brak. "You'll have to forgive his manners. He doesn't have any." She offered her hand to Brak. "I'm Gorva."

"Nice to meet you," Brak replied. Then his eyes grew. "Dragons!"

"Whoa!" Georgio said, pulling his blade in the wink of an eye. "Get behind me! We'll protect you."

Streak, who'd wandered into the area, turned around and asked, "Dragons? Where?"

More dragons from Cinder's brood joined them, surrounding the people in a protective ring.

"I don't see any dragons," Slick said with his gaze toward the sky.

The middling dragon Feather rolled her eyes. "I think they're talking about us."

Cinder approached. His huge frame blocked the moonlight. "What is this warning of dragons? I don't see any."

Dyphestive chuckled. "Feather is right. Our new friends must not be used to dragons. Or at least friendly ones."

"Friendly?" Georgio asked, marveling at the dragons. "As in they won't try to shred us?"

"No, not at all," Dyphestive replied.

"Dragons are rare in our world. Mythical. You have so many," Brak said as he reached out and petted Feather on the head. "You speak like men and are pets?"

"We are more than pets," Feather said. "Friends will do. Would you like to ride the sky, big fella?"

Georgio practically hopped out of his boots. "I would!"

"I don't think that's a good idea," Dyphestive said. "We need to stay close to the tower."

"Ah, it won't hurt." Streak nudged Brak with his nose. "Climb on, big man. I'll take you on a trip you'll never forget."

"I want him to ride on me," Feather said.

"You're too small. Look how big he is." Streak lowered his body.

"I'm not particular," Georgio said. "It would be an honor to ride on a beautiful dragon like you."

"I'll take this one," Feather replied.

A few moments later, Feather and Streak launched into the sky with both men screaming at the top of their lungs. "Wahoo!"

Zora stood by Dyphestive with her arms crossed. "It looks like you made some new companions."

He nodded. "Yeah. I like them."

"Well, I don't," Razor said with a scowl. "Especially the big, scary one. He'd better keep his mitts off my women."

"Put a cork in it, Razor." Gorva slapped him on the behind. "You have more women than you can handle already."

Razor's eyes brightened as he followed Gorva. He said to Zora and Anya with a wink, "No hard feelings, but she's right. There's only so much of me to go around." He took off after Gorva.

"So, how are matters being handled inside that pylon of evil?" Anya asked Dyphestive.

He raised his big shoulders. "I have no idea what they're doing, but they seem to be working hard."

"Good, but it would be best if you kept a close eye on them."

"If you're so worried about it, you go in," Dyphestive said.

"Perhaps I shall." With a snort, Anya grabbed his arm and headed into the tower. "Lead the way."

Anya paced through the Time Mural chamber with her stormy stare grazing over everything in sight.

Grey Cloak and Nath remained seated on the thrones, while Dyphestive sat down on the dais.

"She's very intense, isn't she?" Nath said quietly.

Grey Cloak nodded. He watched Anya pace the room like a hungry panther. It was clear she was out of her comfort zone but was curious at the same time.

She stopped in front of the archway and pushed on the naked wall behind it. "How does this work?"

"You'll see soon enough," Tatiana responded. "Perhaps you should wait outside. You'll be more comfortable since you don't like it here."

"Who said I wasn't comfortable?" Anya asked.

"The air bristles when they speak," Nath said, smiling. He nudged Grey Cloak with his elbow. "Can you feel the tension?"

"I don't think they're meant to get along," he replied.

Anya marched over to the thrones and said, "Tell me more of this plan to invade your home world. I want to go."

"We need to focus on retrieving Gossamer first," Tatiana stated.

Without turning around, Anya said, "I wasn't talking to you. Tell me, Nath. I want to know more."

"Er... well, if you insist. As I was telling Grey Cloak, the recovery of the Thunderstones might allow you to create a weapon that can destroy Black Frost."

"Might?" Grey Cloak asked.

"Well, I can't say it will destroy him with certainty. I only say that it is more powerful than any weapon any of you have ever known." He cleared his scratchy throat. "It is a lethal weapon. Heh-heh."

"Why is that funny?" she asked with a frown.

Nath gave a feeble shrug. "An inside jest. You wouldn't understand. But the Thunderstones have been hidden for a very long time. Guardians protect them. Move them. With my world, Nalzambor, under siege, it is possible there is no one left to guard them at all. I hate to think it, but it is every man and dragon for himself. If there is anything left of any of them."

Anya gave Grey Cloak a serious look. "I'm going."

"We haven't decided who is going yet," Tatiana said. "We only have three collars."

"I'll leave that decision to Grey Cloak." Anya gave him a pressing look. "You'll make the right decision, won't you?"

"Don't I always?" He caught his brother grinning. "For certain, my brother is going. I'm uncertain about the other."

Anya leaned forward and said, "Well, if it's not me, it had better not be that witch."

9

"I THINK IT'S READY. All we need is the sand," Tatiana said. She spread her fingers out over the pedestal's stage and murmured.

Grains of sand rose from between the cracks in the stone floor and gathered together in the air. They spun slowly like a small dust devil.

She knew it was the very sand she'd used when she traveled back and forth from Bish. It had spilled on the floor when Honzur was killed and the Pedestal of Power broken.

The sand floated over the bowl. When she made a pouring motion with her hand, the sand sprinkled over the gemstones.

Tatiana released her spell and took a breath. Datris stood to her right and Dalsay to her left.

"Are you certain that the stones are in their proper positions?" Dalsay asked.

"I was counting on you," she said.

Dalsay's ghostly face paled.

"I'm jesting, my darling," she said. "This is the correct sequence. I've studied it a thousand times."

Grey Cloak stepped toward them and said, "So, we're ready."

"Ready to summon Gossamer back. Yes. But it will be delicate. We cannot say for certain where Georgio and Brak will return, but we hope it is in close proximity." Tatiana beckoned to the pair of otherworlders. "Are you prepared to return?"

Georgio wandered toward the archway and said, "I'm not as eager as I was earlier. Not after riding the dragons and meeting your women. Whoo! Not that the women in Bone aren't fair, but you gals are a might bit prettier." He rubbed his jaw as he checked out Tatiana. "I wish we had elves in our world."

"Well said," Brak agreed.

Datris handed a gem-studded metal collar to Georgio. "Give this to Gossamer the first chance you get. It will immediately return him to us."

"What about the other two? Dirklen and Magnolia," Georgio asked. "Do you want them back?"

"Dragons no," Grey Cloak said. "You can have them."

"Good. Because we're going to put ropes around their

necks and hang them for what they did." Georgio turned and faced his companion. "Brak, are you ready?"

Brak shrugged his burly shoulders. "I suppose. After all, Bish is home."

Grey Cloak and Dyphestive shook hands with the pair of foreigners.

"Thank you for the help," Dyphestive said.

"Thanks for sending us back," Georgio replied. "I only wish we had more time to try the food. Who knows. Maybe next time."

Tatiana nodded and began motioning to the pedestal. "Grey Cloak and Dyphestive, I suggest you stand back."

The blood brothers complied.

Gems inside the archway pulsed with colorful energy. The block in the wall behind the archway shifted and faded to black. Warm wind caressed their faces. A visionary landscape of a dry, barren land appeared. Grey Cloak and Dyphestive split apart.

Georgio and Brak stepped between the brothers. They exchanged glances, gave each other a nod, and jumped into the portal.

A quick, sucking *shaloop* sound like water being drained followed. The men from Bish were gone, but the picture of the bleak landscape remained.

Datris stood by Tatiana's side with his arm around her waist. Sweat beaded on her forehead.

"How long can she keep the portal open?" Grey Cloak asked Dalsay, who hovered by Tatiana's other side.

"Opening the portal is more difficult than keeping it open, but she cannot maintain it for long," Dalsay said solemnly. "It could kill her."

Dyphestive approached the pedestal. "We cannot allow that to happen."

"We are venturing into new waters," Dalsay said. He floated down to the main floor. "I sense she is strong at the moment. If Gossamer doesn't return as we planned, we can close the portal and try again after her strength returns."

Anya paced the room with her arms crossed and said, "We'll spend the rest of our lives wandering these halls, waiting for the wizards to get it right. My skin prickles from all of these delays."

"Zooks, Anya. They only went inside a few moments ago. Don't you think you can be a little more patient?" Dyphestive asked.

With a hand on her hilt, she said, "Don't scold me, pup."

Dyphestive bristled. "Who are you calling pup?"

Grey Cloak moved between them and said, "Everyone, take a breath. It's going to work. It might take some time, but it will work. You must have faith in that."

"Talk some sense into your oafish brother, or I will cut him down like a tree." Anya gave Dyphestive a parting glance and departed from the chamber.

"Oafish? Who is she calling oafish? At least I'm not as moody as a hungry wildcat!" he yelled in her direction.

Anya's voice carried from the deep corridors into the chamber. "I heard that!"

Dyphestive flinched. Then a grin fell upon his face.

"What are you smiling at?" Grey Cloak asked.

"Remember when we first met her and I said I was going to marry her?"

"Yes."

"Well, I changed my mind."

10

BISH

"Bɪsʜ," Georgio muttered. He wiped the sweat on his face with his sleeve and glanced up at the burning suns. "Talk about being dropped in the middle of nowhere. I'm beginning to think we should have stayed in Gapoli. I didn't even see any sand."

Brak trudged along by Georgio's side, arms swinging slowly with his long steps. They'd been walking for a day and a night. "I tend to agree. You could eat the grass there."

Georgio gave his friend a funny look. "You didn't eat the grass, did you?"

"No." Brak's stomach grumbled. "But I'd eat it now."

"Oh no. You're going to try to eat me, aren't you?"

Brak shrugged. "Only if I have to."

"Bone," he muttered.

"No need to curse."

"I'm not cursing. Look!" He pointed at the horizon. Bright castle spires glinted behind the great wall over the next rise. "It's Bone!"

"Sweet mother of Bish! Home!" Brak roared. He started running down the abandoned trail with long strides. "Last man to the gate buys the first ten rounds."

"What?" Georgio laughed with his hands on his hips. "You can't outrun me." His eyes widened. "Oh, he's really moving." He took off at a dead sprint after Brak.

Winded, they wandered through the jaws of the smaller pedestrian entrance with their hands clutching their sides. Brak had won the race by a full thirty paces.

"When did you start running so fast? You're as flat-footed as a goose," Georgio said as he waved at one of the watchmen he knew on the wall.

"I have longer legs," Brak replied.

"Fine. I'm happy to buy."

A watchman handed Georgio a jug of water and asked, "What were you doing out there?"

"Don't ask." Georgio guzzled down some water and poured the rest of the contents over his head. He tossed the empty jug to a befuddled-looking Brak.

"Thanks." Brak handed the watchman the jug. "Grab me another, will you?" He glowered at Georgio. "I ought to make that ten buckets of ale, not mugs."

"Sorry." Georgio grabbed the neck of his damp shirt

and started fanning himself. "Oh, Gossamer. We have to find him!"

They headed toward the Royal Chimera. To their amazement, they found Lefty and the City Watch waiting in the stables across the street.

Lefty Lightfoot jumped off a sawhorse. With his halfling face filled with glee, he said, "You're back! You're back!" He ran and jumped into Georgio's arms and beat on his chest. "What happened? Where have you been?" He shook Georgio by the jerkin. "I want to know everything! I'm chronicling every detail in my records!"

"Easy, Lefty." Georgio plucked the clingy halfling off like a tick. "Where is Gossamer?"

"Oh. He's sleeping."

"No, I'm not." Gossamer emerged from a stable, rubbing his eyes. The elf's black-and-white hair was no longer separated in the middle but in a mess of tangles. His matching robes were practically ribbons. His eyes grew wide when he saw the collar in Georgio's hand. "They did it?"

"I don't know what they did, but we're back." Georgio offered Gossamer the gem-studded collar. "Tatiana said as soon as you put it on, it will bring you home."

"Tatiana?" Gossamer's eyes watered. "She's well." He pulled his hair up and turned around. "Please, put it on. And thank you. All of you!"

"Glad to help. That's what we do. Take care." Georgio snapped the collar around Gossamer's neck.

In a wink, Gossamer vanished.

"That didn't take long," Brak said. He slapped his large hand on Georgio's shoulder. "You owe me some ale."

"We'll get to that." Georgio scanned the stable. "Lefty, where are Dirklen and Magnolia?"

Lefty fastened the brass buttons on his vest. "Melegal took them. They're in the dungeons, heavily guarded, behind bars thicker than Brak's wrist."

Georgio put on his cap and said, "Good, because we're going to hang them tomorrow. But first, we have some ale to drink. It's time to celebrate. Brak and I have been to another world and back again. And wait till you hear about their women."

Grey Cloak sat with his legs dangling over the arm of the pewter throne. His back was to Nath, who remained seated beside him.

It had been hours since Georgio and Brak departed. The wizards remained in place behind the pedestal, as steady as stones, but Tatiana's brow was creasing.

Dyphestive sat on the steps leading up to the thrones with his chin resting in his palm.

Inside the Time Mural was the slowly changing picture of Bish's bleak wilderness. Leagues of dusty roads and mounds of reddened clay made up the ground. Broken trails snaked through the rise. The setting suns bathed the chamber in broad daylight that brought no warmth.

"It's not as bad as it looks," Nath stated.

Grey Cloak shifted in his chair, and Dyphestive turned his head over his shoulder.

"What do you mean?" Dyphestive asked.

"Bish. Those are the Outlands you see. Broken and desolate. But there are grand forests and lands full of wonder." Nath took a breath. "Don't let the ugly crust fool you. It has breathtaking places the same as this world."

"Is Nalzambor anything like Bish?" Dyphestive asked.

Nath raised his shoulders. "Perhaps now. Black Frost takes so much. I'm fearful to see what is left of my world. I have faith, though. I'm certain a remnant still survives."

Dyphestive asked, "You think everyone is dead?"

Frowning, Nath replied, "With the rivers drying up and the lifeless crops, the people will starve. It's inevitable."

"Grey," Dyphestive said, "we can't let that happen. If Gossamer doesn't return soon, perhaps we should under-take our journey to Nath's world."

He nodded and sat up straight. "I've thought about that. I've thought about many things. One way or the other," he said to Nath, "we will go."

"Thank you," Nath said. Suddenly, his golden eyes brightened.

The air in the room stirred.

Gossamer appeared. The disheveled wizard wobbled and fell to his knees. "Lords of Thunder! Thank goodness I have returned!"

11

WIZARD WATCH

GREY CLOAK WAS the first one to embrace Gossamer and welcome him back. "It's good to see you back, friend."

"You as well." Gossamer returned a feeble hug and sighed. "I had my share of doubts as to whether or not I'd see you again." His gaze found Tatiana.

She detached herself from the Pedestal of Power. The Time Mural image of the Outlands faded back into the wall of stone. She eased down the steps and met Gossamer at the base, where they hugged.

"Tatiana, I feared I'd never see you again. Any of you. Black Frost is full of devilish tricks," Gossamer said. He handed her the collar. "This worked well. It appears you're getting closer to mastering the Time Mural."

"When we put it back together, we made some improvements," Tatiana said, managing a smile.

Perplexed, Gossamer asked, "Put it back together? We already rebuilt it once."

"Our guest, Brak, destroyed it when he killed Honzur," Datris replied.

"Ah." Gossamer spotted the blood on the floor. "I'm not sure that I want to know how that ended. So, Honzur and Commander Covis are gone?"

"Both dead," Datris said.

"What of Black Frost? Does he know anything?" Gossamer asked.

"No. All of this has happened quickly," Grey Cloak said. "I believe we are at square one, as we planned, many years ago."

Gossamer's brow knitted, and he nodded. "All are safe? Talon?"

"Most are outside along with the sons and daughters of Cinder," Grey Cloak said.

"What about Zanna?"

"She's trapped in the Nether Realm."

Gossamer's eyebrows rose. "The Nether Realm? Why?"

"Tatiana located the Helm of the Dragons there. We tried to retrieve it and failed. Zanna gave herself as a hostage so we could be free," Grey Cloak said sadly. "But we know she still lives. We need to get her back so that you can send her back in time. Back to Ice Vale, where she found Dyphestive and me with the barbarians."

"She pulled it off," Gossamer muttered.

"What do you mean?"

"Don't you see? Zanna removed herself from us so that she wouldn't cross with herself. Datris and I can still rescue her from Black Frost's temple, bring her here, and send her back. It has all worked perfectly, as she suggested."

"Wait a moment." Grey Cloak didn't hide his disgust. "Are you telling me we're supposed to leave her there? In the Nether Realm with Utlas the speaker?"

"Listen to me. She is safest where she is now. Don't you see? That's why she did what she did." Gossamer offered Grey Cloak a sympathetic look. "When you and Dyphestive were stone, she came back to see me. We played through hundreds of scenarios."

Incredulous, Grey Cloak asked, "You knew this would happen?"

"No, we didn't know anything, but we tried to guess Black Frost's every move. We didn't foresee the Dragon Helm being located in the Nether Realm. However, we did foresee a trap, which Zanna hoped to lead you away from. Datris and I must go to Black Frost quickly. We will swap Datris with her stone statue and bring her back here. I don't think Black Frost will suspect anything at this point, so long as all of you lie low. Stay concealed in the tower, all of you."

"But we know that Black Frost communicates with Utlas. He will tell him of our escape," Dyphestive warned him.

"Possibly," Grey Cloak said. "But from what I saw of Utlas, he might not want to let Black Frost know we escaped. And I think he has his own plans in mind for the Dragon Helm."

Dyphestive replied, "That isn't a very strong plan."

"No, but it will have to hold. What are you going to tell Black Frost about Honzur and Covis?" Grey Cloak asked Gossamer.

"Datris and I will be prepared."

"Before you go, you need to know something. Without the Helm of Dragons, we came up with another plan to destroy Black Frost." Grey Cloak nodded toward the thrones. "This is Nath."

Gossamer bowed. "A pleasure to meet the man I've heard much about."

"He wants us to go to his world to retrieve a weapon capable of destroying Black Frost," Grey Cloak said.

"We're running out of options. You must do what you feel you must do," Gossamer said. "Come, Datris. We must make haste." He embraced Tatiana again. "We shall return soon." He nodded to Dalsay, who nodded back.

Then he and Datris headed out of the chamber and were gone.

Grey Cloak sorted through his thoughts. Zanna was safe, and she wasn't. He didn't know what to make of her actions. Everything she had done was as if she'd known what she was getting into all along and suffered for it anyway. He faced the Time Mural. The fate of his world rested on another world hidden from view behind those stone walls.

"Tatiana, how much rest do you need before you can send us to Nath's world?"

She sat down with her head cradled in her hands. "A day should do it."

Dalsay sat by her side and said, "You need more time than that, my love."

"Perhaps, but we're running out of time. I can feel it. Can't you?"

"Yes."

"We'll let you rest," Grey Cloak said. He tipped his head at Dyphestive. "Come on, brother. Let's check in with the others."

12

THE NETHER REALM

Cords of mystic energy bound Zanna Paydark to a slab of rock that floated in the sky. The stone slowly rotated, and her view shifted from the Flaming Fence, which made a sky and ground of fire, to the humongous palace of the Nether World.

Every time she flipped over, her stomach turned sick. Her tongue was dry, and the bands burned her wrists.

With her eyes closed, she tried to summon her wizard fire and break her chains. But the more she summoned her energy, the tighter and hotter her shackles became.

"Guh!" She banged her head against the stone. Sweat dripped from her face into the pit of fire below. Opening her eyes, she sighed. "Anything for my son."

The hard stone, which made a crude bed, came to a stop and floated upright. She faced Utlas's palace and spotted the giant walking down the wide flight of stone stairs.

Utlas stood on the edge of the cliff, his stare boring into her. Then he stepped onto a similar slab, floated her way, and came to a stop no more than a dozen feet away. Tall and lean, the gaunt giant towered over her by several feet. His slender arms—as smooth and hairless as his head— were crossed over his chest. He wore a ceremonial garment of a priest, but the trim had frayed, and patches in the fabric appeared moth-eaten.

"Enjoying your stay?" Utlas asked. His voice was rich and deep but as gentle as petals on a flower with a touch of mockery.

Zanna tried to blow away a damp strand of dark hair hanging over her eye, shrugged, and said, "I have to tell you, Utlas. I don't follow your logic about my location. If I fall into the Flaming Fence, I'll be free."

His sunken cheeks tightened. He massaged his high cheekbones with a thumb and finger. "It sounds as if you're planning your escape."

"No different from you. But I've passed through the flames. You can't."

"Yes, well, I've come to terms with my situation. But I believe there will be change soon enough. Besides, now that you've joined us, you need to feel as we do." Utlas stretched his long arm over the horizon of flames. "You see the path to freedom, yet you can never escape. It's torment, isn't it?"

"I don't know, but I don't plan on being here as long as you've been."

"We'll see about that." He started to turn away.

"What are your plans, Utlas? You can't escape without the help of Black Frost. And you can't tell Black Frost about your failure."

He turned and squared his shoulders. "Failure?"

"You might have the Helm of the Dragons and me, but you let his archenemies go." She tossed her head back and laughed, her head cracking against the stone. "Oh, that hurt. But it's still funny. I can help you, Utlas. No one knows Black Frost better than I do."

"Our relationship is strong. Black Frost trusts me."

"I've seen Black Frost in action over the past few decades. You haven't. No one who has failed him survived. If you tell him you let Grey Cloak loose, he'll turn the Flaming Fence against all of you. That will be it, one way or the other."

Utlas stiffened. "What do you propose, Zanna Paydark?"

"To start, I really need to relieve myself. Can we talk after that? It won't take long, but I'm about to burst." She gave him a friendly smile. "All you need to do is keep me away from the Flaming Fence. There's no way for me to escape otherwise. And I'll keep my business quick."

His wrinkled lips twisted, then he grumbled and said, "Very well."

Yes!

"How do you like my estate?" Utlas asked.

Zanna stood in a massive study. Ancient wooden shelving ran along the walls from top to bottom, covered in dust. Cobwebs hung in the corners, and the shelves were mostly barren. Ugly little black bugs ran along the edges.

"It's better than I would have imagined." She paced the vast room, searching high and low. Finely woven rugs had holes in them. Her steps were short, as the mystic shackles on her ankles and wrists limited her mobility. She tested them. Any sudden moves, and they would tighten and drain her. Regardless, it felt good to move again. That small bit of freedom gave her hope. "Clearly when it was built, there were better intentions."

Utlas returned a smug smile. He sat behind a desk built for a giant. It stood on four legs made of tremendous thigh bones, and the top was solid black marble. He tapped his fingertips together and said, "When we were banished, we thought we could still conquer the world. No Flaming Fence was going to keep us down. Using the materials and knowledge at our disposal, together, we created a majestic city. All of us were focused on proving those who would exile us to be wrong. With a hearty spirit, we thrived. As you can see, the Nether Realm was once nothing short of glorious."

Zanna distanced herself from the four soldiers of the condemned who'd escorted her into the room. Their gargoyle-like skin was so thick that it was difficult to tell whether they had been men, orcs, or elves at one time. They carried spears with ugly, razor-sharp heads that were the only objects in the room that shone.

She made herself comfortable on an iron chair with a black velvet seat that was torn. She tried to cross her legs but couldn't. "So, what happened?"

Utlas sighed. "Once we achieved all we wished to achieve, our sense of purpose and nobility declined, replaced by our moral depravity instead.

She nodded.

Keep him talking. He needs to show me the Helm of the Dragons.

"Tell me more. I'm interested."

"The arrangement was for you to help me deal with Black Frost."

She shrugged and asked, "What's the hurry? After all, I'd like to learn a little more about you first."

He drummed his fingers on the table and said, "How refreshing."

13

DOVERUN

SORENESS AND BURNING SEEPED through Bowbreaker's skin, down into the bones. The Golden Sentries hadn't eased their punishment of him. The crack of a whip still sounded in his ears, and he was still bleeding.

Sitting doubled over on a stone bench, he sat up and groaned. The wounds on his back, which were caked with blood, opened again, and another burning sensation flowed through his limbs.

He'd been brought into another holding cell similar to the dungeons but not quite the same. The cell was near the arena, where the stench of death reigned. He wasn't alone in his suffering either.

"How are you holding up?" Commander Christo asked. The older elven soldier had been punished as badly as

Bowbreaker. His lips were cracked open, and his face was bruised and swollen.

Trying to maintain strength in his voice, Bowbreaker replied, "It will take a lot more than the snap of leather to break me."

Christo let out a rusty *heh-heh*. "For whatever it's worth, I am honored to fight by your side one last time, Bowbreaker. I know you were on the right side of things. Perhaps I can redeem myself for being so blind and foolish. I let duty blind me from the truth." He lifted the shackles and chains on his wrists. "Look how it repaid me."

"There is no wrong in serving your country. We're soldiers. We do what we do. In today's world, it's difficult to tell who's right and who's wrong."

"It's clear who is wrong." Christo sat up and leaned his back against the wall. The wooden doors at the top of the stairs, which led outside, were vibrating. "Hear that? The crowd is awakened. Their hungry murmurings shake the doors. It's not often they see the abominations let loose, though it has been more recent of late."

"You say they come from the abyss?" Bowbreaker asked. As a ranger, he was familiar with all sorts of the world's creatures, but the abominations Christo spoke of were a mystery to him. "Can you tell me more? You've seen them?"

"They're different. Sometimes they send one, other times two or more. They devour men whole." Christo pursed his lips and exhaled. "In all my years, I've never seen the likes of them. Parts of many creatures, all in one. As I said, abominations."

"Perhaps if I understood more, we could defeat them."

Christo rocked his shoulders back and forth, and with a sparkle in his eye, he said, "That's why I delight in dying with you. You believe we have a fighting chance, but I assure you, we don't."

Bowbreaker gave him a hard look and said, "Is that how you'll fight your final battle? With doubt?"

"No, I have no doubt. We will die, but I promise to make a fight out of it." Christo raised his arms and shook his chains. "I only hope they remove the shackles. Not that it matters to them. The abominations can eat them."

"I think you're telling tall tales," Bowbreaker said. "Creatures don't eat metal. Not even dragons."

"If you say so."

The entrance doors opened, and soldiers shoved more prisoners into the room. The prisoners, two male and two female elves, were stripped down to their underclothes. They were forced down to their knees at spearpoint.

"Enjoy your deaths, traitors," one of the soldiers said.

He and the two others backed out of the room and sealed all the prisoners inside.

"It seems we won't have to suffer alone. We have company." Christo squinted. "Though I don't recognize them."

"Of course you don't, venerable one," a woman said as

she stood. "We're not West River elves like you. We come from the east." She turned her attention to Bowbreaker. "We come to aid our brother, the rightful king, Bowbreaker."

Bowbreaker's jaw dropped, and he asked, "Adana?"

Adana bowed. She was strong, well-built, with attractive angular features like Bowbreaker. "Yes, brother, it is I."

He got to his feet and embraced her in a strong hug. Hers was just as fierce. "What have you done? What are you doing here?"

"Trying to kill Queen Esmarelda. We've been spying on her for a long time." Adana stepped aside and motioned to her companions. This is Sheela, my right hand," she said, pointing at a lovely young elf with short hair the color of ravens' feathers. She nodded at a stern-looking younger man with flowing brown hair and an older blond elf with a wild look in his eyes. "These are Archbow and Raghan. We've come to join you."

"In death?" Christo asked with whimsy.

Bowbreaker shook hands with the other elves. "It is my pleasure to meet all of you." He turned his gaze on his sister and asked, "But why are you here? Were you captured? Do they know—"

"That I'm your sister? No. When we learned that you were captured, we allowed them to capture us. Is it true you could have killed Esmarelda?"

"I was as close as I am to you, but I couldn't do it. Not in cold blood."

Adana raised an eyebrow. "You don't still love her, do you?"

"Of course not. She is dunked in darkness. My skin crawls in her presence." He shook his head. "I cannot explain why I didn't act, but I feel I did what was right. But, Adana, why would you not flee? Queen Esmarelda plans to attack the East River elves and wipe them out."

"I know."

"Why didn't you warn the others?"

"Because, brother, I was more worried about you."

14

LED through the tunnels of the arena by the Golden Sentries, Bowbreaker said to his sister, "I admit, Adana, I'm perplexed as to your reasoning." His jaw muscles clenched. "There is no reason to share my fate."

"There is every reason." She walked side by side with him, rubbing shoulders in the narrow corridor. "You're my brother, and we're your servants. We must stand by the side of the true and rightful king."

"Silence!" The soldiers punched both of them in their bellies with the butt ends of their spears. "Save your strength for screaming for mercy."

Bowbreaker doubled over, and his sister fell to her knees. He helped her back to her feet and eyed his captors.

"Don't try to stare me down, assassin," a Golden Sentry said. He sneered at Bowbreaker. "I'll put a hole clean through you if I have to. Queen Esmarelda has given us the authority to do so if you resist."

Bowbreaker dropped his gaze.

"Good. You're wise enough to live a little longer, but if it were up to me, I'd finish you now. I wouldn't make a spectacle of it," the Golden Sentry said. He turned his hard stare on Commander Christo. "You disappoint me, Christo. I'm sorry to see you die in the company of these wretches."

"Sergeant Saltun, you know as well as I that I don't deserve this. But if it is my fate, I accept it." Christo stood up to his full height and said, "Queen Esmarelda is an agent of evil. Even you must know that."

"I only know one thing—my duty," Sergeant Saltun replied. "That is all that matters." He gave Christo a hard shove in the back. "Get inside."

The prisoners were pushed into another room that had a wooden gate. Sergeant Saltun closed a set of barred metal doors.

Another soldier tossed in a large set of metal pliers.

"Use those to remove the shackles," Sergeant Saltun said. "You might want to hang on to the metal, though. It might be the only weapon you have." Wickedness glinted in his eyes. "Not that it will do you any good. But I'd hurry. Those doors will open at any moment."

Archbow grabbed the pliers and started twisting the bolts out of the screws on Bowbreaker's chains.

"Take care of Adana and yourselves first," Bowbreaker said. "No shackle will hold me when the time comes."

Sergeant Saltun offered a mocking grin and said, "You should have used that great strength to begin with." He huffed and addressed the other Golden Sentries. "Don't let them come close to those bars. If they do, run them through."

As Archbow twisted the nuts from the shackles, Bowbreaker listened to the murmurings growing outside the door. The crowd began to chant Bowbreaker's name, and the noise grew louder.

"They call for my death," Bowbreaker said.

"Well, you aren't dead yet," the wild-eyed Raghan said. He snatched the pliers from Archbow. "Let me have those claws." He twisted the nuts away from the threads, quickly removing them all. "That's better. What are you waiting for Sheela? An invitation?"

Sheela stepped over to Raghan and let him unfasten the shackles then gathered one set of chains and slung it over her shoulder. She grabbed another set and spun it like a sling and gave an approving nod.

"They said this abomination eats metal. Well, I'll give it a mouthful if it wants," Raghan said as he draped his chains over his neck and shoulders.

The wooden door groaned and started to lower like a drawbridge.

Adana exchanged glances with Sheela, then they

rushed toward the bars and banged on them. "Let us out, please! Spare us!" they shouted.

Two Golden Sentries pointed their spears at them.

"Get back!" one said. "You've sealed your fate!"

They took jabs at them through the bars.

The elven women sidestepped the weapons and grabbed the spears by the top of the shaft. Each bracing one foot against the bars, they yanked.

"Aargh!"

The Golden Sentries' faces slammed into the metal bars, but they held on.

Bowbreaker and Archbow burst into action, grabbing separate spears and ripping them from the soldiers' grasps.

Steel scraped out of sheaths. Adana and Sheela had reached through the bars and robbed both soldiers' swords and daggers from their belts. They sauntered backward with winning smiles on their faces and joined the men.

In a moment, they'd stripped the soldiers of two spears, two long swords, and two daggers.

"You give those back!" one of the soldiers shouted.

"Come inside and get them, fools," Adana said. "What's the matter? Are you too frightened to join us on the field of battle against the abomination?"

One of the elven soldiers spit through the bars. "It doesn't matter. All of you are dead either way!"

Adana thumbed the edge of her sword. "Perhaps, but

thanks to you, we have a much better chance than we had before."

"Well played, sister," Bowbreaker said. "I hope you have more tricks up your sleeve."

She glanced at her bare arms and said, "I wish I could say I did, but this is the best I can do."

He tapped his spear on the ground. "Then it will be enough."

The door dropped with a loud *wham*.

The crowd stood, stomping and screaming. Pumping their fists toward the sky, they shouted, "Bowbreaker! Bowbreaker! Bowbreaker!"

"After you, brother," Adana said.

He nodded and stepped out into the full light of day.

The stands exploded in a chorus of life-threatening cheers.

Raghan joined Bowbreaker's side. "You really are popular," he quipped. "But in a bad sort of way."

15

WIZARD WATCH

TATIANA SNAPPED one of the collars around Grey Cloak's neck. "I suggest you don't remove it. We will summon you back at any time, and our time line will not be the same as one in another world."

"What does that mean?" Dyphestive asked as Datris tried to snap a collar around his neck. Datris ended up hooking it into place above the nook in Dyphestive's elbow.

"If only it were easy to explain," Tatiana said as she adjusted the gem-studded collar on Grey Cloak's neck. "Time in our world might be faster than the one in your world. I experienced it when I went to Bish. These worlds are not perfectly aligned. Using the pedestal, we try to manage that the best that we can."

Dyphestive scratched his chin. "So, you are saying days here could be hours there?"

Tatiana nodded.

"This is going to be interesting." Grey Cloak ran a finger under his collar. "And uncomfortable."

"I would go, but my expertise is needed to manage the Time Mural." She grabbed Grey Cloak's finger. "And I made some adjustments. Feel this large gem. If you find what you're looking for, press it, and you will return here." She moved back to the pedestal, where Dalsay waited. "Are you ready?"

Grey Cloak looked at his brother, and they both shrugged. "No sense in wasting any more time. We must do what we must do before Black Frost sniffs us out."

"Even if he does, we still have time on our side to start," Tatiana said as she began adjusting the gemstones. "There are six towers, but they all work as one. He would have to destroy all of them to stop us."

"That seems impossible," Grey Cloak said. "Our chances are looking better already."

"The towers were designed with such a purpose in mind," she said. "It was your father's idea. It was the best way to ensure our survival. The only sure way to defeat us is from within, and the underlings were able to do that. But if a tower topples, the others will shake and weaken."

"Fascinating," Nath said as he rose from the throne and joined them in front of the archway. His scaly fingers reached into his shirt, and he withdrew a gold ring that hung from a leather cord. It had two small gemstones, an emerald and a ruby, that appeared like eyes in the head of a dragon. He gave it to Dyphestive. "This is my signet ring. My allies will know it, and it will help you find the Thunderstones."

Dyphestive looped the necklace over his head and tucked it into his shirt. "I'll take care of it."

"I'm going to need something from your world in order to make a connection," Tatiana said to Nath.

"I know." Nath produced a lock of his hair that was bound up with a leather tie and tossed it to her. "This should do." He eyed Grey Cloak. "I hate cutting my hair, but a dragon has to do what a dragon has to do."

"Will we be able to use our magic in your world?" Grey Cloak asked.

"You can only hope what works here will still work there." Nath pinched the Cloak of Legends. "A precious garment indeed. But don't rely on it." He eyed both of them. "Rely on your wits. They're what matter most."

Dyphestive went back to the dais and picked up the Iron Sword from the steps.

Nath eyed it with admiration. "A fine length of steel. I had a cherished blade as well. A true friend. Oh." He reached into his belt, took out a strip of parchment, and unrolled it. "This is a map of Nalzambor." He pointed his sharp yellow finger at a particular spot. "This is Dragon Home, also known as the Mountain of Doom. This is where you need to go to find the guardian of the stones."

The brothers kneeled and leaned over the map.

"It's a vast world," Dyphestive said as he gawped at the colorful and well-detailed map. "You drew this?"

Nath shrugged. "I'm good at many things."

A sharp voice interrupted their meeting. "What's happening here?" Anya asked.

They all stood, and Grey Cloak picked up the map and rolled it up.

Zora and Streak followed Anya into the chamber.

"We were about to leave."

"Not without us," Anya, Zora, and Streak said in unison.

Streak moved in front of the women and faced Grey Cloak. "Don't think for a moment that you can leave without me, brother. Uh-uh!"

Grey Cloak put his hand on his dragon's snout and said, "We don't have a collar big enough for your neck."

Streak shoved him back and said, "Make one!"

16

GREY CLOAK STOOD on his knees with his hands on his hips, catching his breath. Traveling through the Time Mural had sucked the life out of him.

They were in a field of brown grass. Leafless trees covered in black bark could be seen over the nearest rise. The sunlight was dimmed by thick, rolling clouds.

"Well, is everyone happy?" Grey Cloak asked.

"I'm queasy," Zora said. She lay on her back, looking up at the sky. "And the world is spinning."

"You wanted to come," Grey Cloak replied.

"I feel fantastic," Streak said. He nodded, stretched his wings, and put his nose to the ground, sniffing. "It doesn't smell much different from our world. It's not as pretty, though."

Grey Cloak said to his brother, "I take it you've never felt better."

"You would be correct," Dyphestive replied as he slowly spun around.

Anya tied her sun-bleached auburn hair into a ponytail. "This place is desolate. I've never seen grass like this." She picked a handful and crushed it. "It crumbles."

All of them had collars on their necks, aside from Streak and Dyphestive. Streak's was above his ankle. Datris and Gossamer revealed that they'd made more collars when in the service of Honzur and Commander Covis and kept them hidden. In the meantime, while the heroes were gone, they planned to make more.

"Our world will be in the same predicament if we don't stop Black Frost. He's draining this world, and our world will be next." Grey Cloak stood and dusted off his knees, looking around. "We need to figure out where we are."

"How are we going to do that?" Zora asked.

"There should be people. Cities. Once we find them, we'll know where we are and can follow the map Nath gave Dyphestive." He eyed the sky and tried to figure out where the sun was. "Shall we go north? South?"

Streak flapped his wings. "I have an idea. Since I'm a dragon, and I can fly, why don't we take a dragon's-eye view of things? After all, wandering aimlessly sounds like a waste of time."

"Fine, Streak and I will go," Anya said.

"Hold on. He's my dragon," Grey Cloak replied.

"Do you wish to double up with me?"

"No."

"How about you, Dyphestive?" Anya asked.

Dyphestive raised a palm. "I'll pass."

"Zora?"

"No, I'll stay here and protect the boys," Zora quipped.

"So be it." Anya climbed into Streak's saddle.

Streak gave Grey Cloak a pleading look, but Grey Cloak just shrugged.

"All right, then. Up, up, and—"

"No, wait," Dyphestive said as he jogged over to Streak and Anya and gave them the map. "You'll need this. And you have to be wary of the skies. Nalzambor has its own breed of dragons. They seek sanctuary on land and in the sky. They aren't the same dragons we know."

Anya put on her helmet and looked down. "Go on. You have my attention."

"You have all of our attention," Grey Cloak said.

"The dragons of Nalzambor have many breeds and sizes. All of them have different powers and abilities," Dyphestive continued. "There are gray-scalers, green lilies, golden flares, fire bites, ivory sliders, silver shades, bull dragons, coppers, uh... the flying fortress."

"Flying fortress? That sounds like Black Frost," Streak

said. He spread out his wings and winked at Dyphestive. "Don't worry about us. We'll be careful."

Anya dug her heels into the stirrups and said in her commanding voice, "Ride the Sky!"

Streak took off running across the field. His talons rose from the ground, and up into the dreary sky they went.

Gazing upward, Zora said, "For such a beautiful woman, Anya sure can be prickly. I can feel myself breathing more easily already."

"Be careful what you say. You know Dyphestive is in love with her," Grey Cloak said.

Dyphestive frowned. "You had to mention that, didn't you?"

Zora giggled. "I forgot about that. It seems like forever ago. Back in Monarch City. Life was much simpler then."

"Agreed."

Streak and Anya became a spot among the clouds. Not long after, they were gone.

Flummoxed, Grey Cloak asked Dyphestive, "When did you and Nath talk about all this?"

"We talk a lot when you aren't around."

"Does he have something against me?"

"No. I can't explain it, but Nath and I have a natural rapport. It happens."

Grey Cloak nodded. "So it does. I'm glad of it, brother. Now, let's head into those hills and see if we can find our own bearings. After all, we can't let Streak and Anya have all the glory."

They marched across the open plains toward the high forest hills looming on the horizon. No birds sang. A land that should have been alive with abundant wildlife was dead.

At the top of the hill, they stepped beneath the dying branches and made their way into the barren woodland.

Many tall trees had crashed to the ground long ago, branches scattered. Brittle twigs snapped underneath their feet like small bones.

Grey Cloak peeled a large hunk of black bark from one tree. Little white worms scurried from the light and vanished into tiny holes.

"Not everything is dead. Some sort of maggot is still thriving."

Zora made a sour face. "Did you have to say that?"

"Say what?" He smirked. "Maggot? You know, if we get hungry, we might not have a better choice."

She punched him in the shoulder. "Don't say that. You'll make me gag."

Chuckling, Grey Cloak led the way through the land of rotting timbers, climbing toward the top of the hill. He navigated around tremendous boulders covered in patches of brown-green moss.

Finally, they arrived at the top and looked down into the valley on the western side.

Grey Cloak pointed at a small establishment of buildings nested in the valley. Small stone cottages had smoke coming from their chimneys. "It looks like we might be able to find our bearings on our own after all. Our fortune has turned." He started down the hill.

With a doubtful expression, Zora said, "Or it may have gotten worse."

17

DOVERUN

THE WOODEN GATE lifted behind Bowbreaker and his comrades and sealed shut. They stood underneath a bright, cloudless sky.

The battle arena was a fifty-yard long oval surrounded by built-in stone seating that was packed full of shouting elves. By the thousands, they screamed like bloodthirsty wolves. Bowbreaker had never seen his people that way except in battle.

Adana and her comrades exchanged uneasy glances.

"They are raving," Adana said, aghast. "What has become of our people?"

"It's a shame," Bowbreaker said as he surveyed the arena.

The oval wall stood over fifteen feet high. At the top

were tight rows of iron rods poking out, making it nearly impossible to climb over.

Black Guard soldiers wearing chain mail under maroon tunics with the Dark Mountain crest were posted on top of the wall. They carried spears that were long enough to stick between barriers of iron rods, a perfect defense against anyone's escape plan.

Bowbreaker moved forward, using his spear like a walking stick. He met eyes with Queen Esmarelda, who sat above the wall on the opposite side of the arena. The stunning elven woman wore a chain-mail dress, and piles of gorgeous hair hung over her shoulders. She was surrounded by a host of Golden Sentries, whose armor shone in the sun. A colorful striped canopy shielded the queen and some of her men from the rays.

Her eyes never left Bowbreaker's as a Golden Sentry commander who sat beside her leaned over while she spoke into his ear.

The commander stood and motioned for Bowbreaker and his companions to come forward.

As one, the group walked across the dusty, bloodstained ground and stopped when the commander held his hand up, glowering down at them. He raised his arms and dropped them, and the crowd quieted.

"Tell me"—the commander leaned over the wall—"where did you acquire those weapons?"

"Don't you recognize them?" Adana asked. She skillfully flipped a well-crafted longsword over her wrist. "It's one of yours. A donation from your precious Golden Sentries."

The commander's brow knitted. The creases in his handsome, angular features deepened. "You will surrender your weapons now."

Christo stepped forward. "Cowards! You have given us a certain death. For none have ever escaped the battle arena! But you won't allow a fighting chance?" He glared at the elven commander. "Shame on you, Commander Roddley!" He jabbed his finger at the elf. "I thought I taught you better." He pointed at the others. "I taught all of you better! And there you all stand, compliant, as the innocent are to be slaughtered!"

"Commander Christo, you of all people know that we are bound by our duty. A duty that you abandoned. But I do not stand before you to negotiate," Commander Roddley said. "I am the voice of the queen. Abandon your weapons. Toss them aside now."

Bowbreaker caught the playful smile on Queen Esmarelda's lips. She enjoyed watching her enemies squirm. His frown deepened, and he looked away.

Commander Christo kept up his tirade. He lifted his sword over his head and yelled to the people in the stands. "Who wants a fair fight? Steel against monster! A battle royal for all to remember! Let them hear your voices!"

An elf in the crowd stood and started a chant. "We want weapons! We want weapons! Weapons!"

Christo led the chorus, pumping his sword in rhythm. "We want weapons! We want weapons!"

Commander Roddley nodded to his sentries. "Archers."

Four archers posted behind the canopy unslung their bows and moved down beside their commander. The dark-eyed, dark-haired elves wore leather armor dyed black and were known as the queen's marksmen. They slid arrows out of their quivers in a quick motion, as smooth as silk, and nocked them on their bowstrings.

Bowbreaker's jaw tightened as the bowmen took aim at Christo.

"Commander Christo! Stop your nonsense!" Commander Roddley warned him. "Discard your weapon, or the archers will take you down!"

"We want weapons!" Christo shouted as he glared back at Commander Roddley. "We want weapons!"

Bowbreaker's skin prickled as he watched the bowmen draw their strings farther back. "Christo, do as he says!" he shouted.

The elder elf continued his feverish tirade, and the supporting crowd grew louder.

Commander Roddley raised his first two fingers and casually dropped his hand. Four bowstrings snapped as one.

Arrows streaked through the air and struck Christo in the center of his chest.

Christo staggered backward, fighting to keep his footing. His sword arm dropped, and he fell back.

A hush fell over the crowd.

Bowbreaker rushed to Christo's side and fell to his knees.

Christo fought for his last breaths as he said, "It's better this way. Better than facing the beast. I'm sorry."

"Don't be. Your last stand was a brave one. You stood for what's right."

Christo nodded. He let out a ragged sigh, and life left his eyes.

Bowbreaker rose and found the queen's marksmen aiming new arrows at him. He tossed the spear aside and stared down the queen. "If this is the slaughter you want to see, so be it."

18

ADANA and her group joined Bowbreaker's side.

"I'd rather fight with my bare hands and feet than die at the hands of a coward's arrow," she said. She tossed her sword and dagger. "I hope that makes the West River elves happy."

Sheela threw her weapons to the ground, as did Archbow and Raghan.

"The greater the odds are against us, the more impressive our victory will be," Raghan said. He slapped his hand down on Bowbreaker's broad shoulder. "Right?"

Bowbreaker dipped his chin. "Queen Esmarelda, if it is to be a fight, let it be a fight in which the combatants have a chance. Look around. There is nowhere for us to go."

Queen Esmarelda stood and came down the stairs,

dragging her chain-mail dress behind her. "Why, my dearest Bowbreaker, all you had to do was ask." She sat down on the edge of the wall. "Go ahead. Take your weapons. After all, I am a fair queen. Let's give *my* people the show they want."

Commander Roddley gave a disapproving frown and said, "But we slew Commander Christo."

"Eh." She shrugged. "He was dead anyway."

"You are a black-hearted witch!" Bowbreaker cried.

"Oh, such emotion. How unexpected from you, my former betrothed. I wish I'd seen more of that passion long ago." Her smile was as enticing as her figure. "But be warned. You might want to control your outburst. I'm a fickle woman and apt to change my mind."

Raghan was the first to pick up a spear. "You don't have to tell me twice.

Commander Roddley nodded at the archers. "Keep your aim on them. If they so much as flinch in our direction, shoot."

Bowbreaker joined the others in picking up the discarded weapons, then they slowly backed away from the wall.

"Goodbye, Bowbreaker," Queen Esmarelda said as she moved away from the wall. "What we had could have been so easy. So great. It might not have turned out how I wished, but at least you kept me entertained." She nodded at her commander. "It's time to let loose the beast." She took her place in her seat, keeping her gaze fastened on Bowbreaker.

Commander Roddley moved to a higher position on the stairs and addressed the crowd. "The time has come! The time you have been waiting for!" He turned his back to the crowd and pointed toward the other end of the arena. "Release Rahdeen the Abomination!"

Bowbreaker and company moved to the middle of the arena and faced the entrance.

The multitudes in the stands pumped their arms in the air and shouted as one. "Rahdeen! Rahdeen! Rahdeen!"

Raghan chanted with them. "Rahdeen! Rahdeen!" He caught everyone in his group giving him a funny look and said, "Sorry, but I'm prone to getting caught up in the moment."

"So, brother, in all your adventures, tell me you've defeated an abomination before," Adana said.

Gripping his spear he replied, "The truth is I've never seen one."

"Neither have I." She took a deep breath and shook her sword and dagger. "Today, we meet one together. And you've killed dragons, right? How much worse could an abomination be?"

Black Guard soldiers stood on the wall above the gate with a bloodthirsty throng behind them chanting, "Open the gate! Open the gate!"

The soldiers turned a wheel of chains mounted in the

stands. The metal door descended like a drawbridge. An immense figure crouched in the shadows.

Quiet fell over the crowd, who craned their necks and leaned over the ledge of the wall. Soldiers pushed the people back.

Rahdeen the Abomination crawled out of its holding cell.

Bowbreaker had never seen anything like the hulking beast. It moved slowly, like a lumbering ape. It pounded the sandy ground with its knuckles. Its oval head was wide and covered in thick scales like a dragon and had an ebony crust of ridges. The beast's four eyes were that of a serpent, as black as pits and penetrating. The nose was nothing more than a pair of nostrils. Fins ran down from its skull and merged with a long, serpentine tail. Saliva dripped from its mouthful of razor-sharp teeth and dripped into puddles on the ground. Grotesque and muscular, it started to rise.

The beast stood twice the height of an average man, and its bulging muscles flexed every time it moved. It stood on a pair of powerful, thick legs. A second pair of arms protruded from its ribs, each ending in a single talon, like a hoof shaved down to a point.

The neckless thing raised its head and shrieked at the bright sky.

The audience cowered and covered their ears.

They weren't alone. Bowbreaker's comrades grimaced,

yet they stood their ground. He studied the creature, searching for a weakness.

"I don't know what black pit that thing crawled out of, but I'm starting the think eating an arrow might have been the better choice," Raghan said.

Bowbreaker nodded. "Agreed. But there will be no turning back now. Everyone, spread out."

As soon as the company moved, the abomination charged with startling speed.

19

OTHER THAN A DRAGON, Bowbreaker had never seen a creature so large move so fast.

"Spread out!" he commanded.

The prisoners scattered in all directions.

The abomination swung its massive head around and set its hungry gaze on Sheela. It dashed after the young elven woman, who sprinted away.

Like a wolf chasing a rabbit in an open field, the abomination closed in on the fleet-footed elf with its jaws wide open. Its fist unfolded, revealing long, bony fingers with nails like talons. It struck out, and Sheela jumped left, rolled, and sprinted back toward the middle of the arena.

The others moved back toward the wall, keeping their distance, but waved their arms at the monster.

"Over here, Ugly!" Archbow said with his sword flashing above his head. "Try to take a bite out of me!"

The wild-eyed audience exploded with deafening roars.

"Sheela," Bowbreaker called. He readied his spear on his shoulder. "Come to me!"

With her face a mask of concentration, Sheela ran away from Bowbreaker with the abomination on her heels. Then she pivoted, ducked under its slashing claws, and darted back toward Bowbreaker, who moved toward the middle of the arena.

The abomination skidded toward the wall, clawing the earth, and turned back in pursuit.

Bowbreaker studied the hard scales, searching for a weakness. It had to have a soft spot somewhere. Every creature, no matter how formidable, had a flaw.

Sheela closed in on his position, and Rahdeen's long strides allowed him to close in on her. Fifty feet. Forty feet. Thirty feet.

Bowbreaker hurled his spear. It sailed straight and true, threatening to gore the monster's skull like a pumpkin.

The abomination shifted to one side, and the spear pierced the meat of its shoulder.

It stopped in its tracks, opened its jaws, and shrieked to the heavens. Using its free hand, it grabbed the spear and ripped it out. The spear tip was coated with oily blood.

"It bleeds!" Raghan shouted with jubilation. He charged toward the monster's backside.

Archbow attacked with him.

"Brethren, no!" Bowbreaker shouted.

Both elves arrived at the same time. Raghan stabbed the monster in the back of the knee, and Archbow hacked into the brute's tendons on the opposite leg.

The abomination's tail cracked like a bullwhip, striking Raghan and flipping him head over heels toward the wall. It twisted at the hips, snatched up Archbow in its powerful talons, and lifted him high above the ground. It's bottom arms punched the life out of Archbow's body.

"No!" Adana screamed. Her eyes teared as the monster cast aside Archbow's limp body.

Raghan lay against the wall, not moving.

Only three elves were left standing against the monster.

Bowbreaker watched in horror as the wound in the abomination's shoulder closed in moments.

The audience stood clapping, screaming, and stomping.

In a matter of seconds, Rahdeen had taken down two formidable elves. It wouldn't take longer to finish the others.

Bowbreaker stood weaponless and with no idea how to kill the creature. He, Adana, and Sheela had formed a triangle around the monster. He nodded at both of them and said, "We need to buy time."

"How do we do that?" Adana asked.

"Run."

As soon as he finished the word, the abomination charged him.

Bowbreaker could run like the wind for hours, as could most elves. But what they didn't know was how long the beast could keep up. The abomination's strides were longer, and it moved almost as fast.

Cutting one way then the other, Bowbreaker kept his companions out of harm's way. He angled back to the spot where Archbow had fallen and snatched up his sword.

Adana called to him, "What do you want us to do, brother?"

"Find a weakness. It's the only way."

Sheela moved toward Raghan's body, picked up his spear, and guarded the fallen man.

Like his feet, Bowbreaker's mind raced. He'd been trained since childhood on the various ways to slay creatures of all sorts. All of them had weaknesses. But the abomination had rock-hard plating that looked like a suit of iron armor over its chest. Its skull looked as thick as stones. It obviously had armor that no weapon could pierce.

Regardless, Bowbreaker had to stop it—or die.

He turned toward the monster, and it overshot him, flailing its arms, and its spiked hands struck the dirt.

Bowbreaker sliced open one of the monster's palms then sidestepped and chopped off three of its toes. He jumped out of reach as the abomination pursued.

It stumbled on its wounded foot and released a savage cry. Oily blood spit out of the wound until it closed, and the nubs of new toes started to grow.

The elven steel Bowbreaker carried was as sharp as a razor and hard to break. It was as good a weapon as any without being enchanted.

He sprinted toward Adana. "I have a strategy."

"I can see that. It limps," she replied.

"Only so long as it cannot heal. We can't let that happen," he warned her.

She gave him a firm nod. "I know what to do." She lifted her sword and charged, shouting, "For Bowbreaker!"

20

"Commander Roddley"—Queen Esmarelda leaned forward—"do my eyes deceive me? It appears the prisoners are very much alive instead of dead."

The elven commander's eyes were fastened on the battle in the arena. He gulped. "Your Majesty, the weapons you supplied them with have only delayed their inevitable demise. Rahdeen the Abomination cannot be killed. It's only a matter of time."

Inside the arena, Bowbreaker hacked off the beast's foot. Down on one knee, it battled the attacking elves like a cornered dog.

Commander Roddley, struggling to be heard above the noise of the crowed, added, "The elves will tire. No one can keep up that effort. They'll die soon."

"You'd better be right," the queen said. "I'd hate to be embarrassed."

"Bowbreaker is not going anywhere. We have more soldiers than he has hairs on his head. Even if the abomination fails to kill him, the Golden Sentries won't."

A fierce backswing from the abomination caught Sheela in the back and sent her sprawling face-first to the ground.

The queen jumped out of her seat. "Kill her, Rahdeen! Slay her now!"

Rahdeen's tail flipped up and came down hard across Sheela's back. Sheela let out a scream.

Commander Roddley grinned at the queen and nodded.

Queen Esmarelda dropped back down in her seat, grinding her teeth. "Only two left standing. I want Bowbreaker saved for last. I want him to suffer."

As the beast's tail pounded Sheela into the ground, Bowbreaker spun away from the monster's grip and sliced off the tail.

Adana grabbed Sheela's limp body and dragged it away. Then with sword and dagger in hand, she resumed her attack.

Bowbreaker moved toward the beast with his sword flashing back and forth. He cut off the tips of the abomination's fingers in one stroke. A second swipe took off an arm.

With both hands raising her sword high, Adana rushed

toward Rahdeen, then she cut deep into its shoulder. She continued to hack until the flesh opened.

The monster screamed, flailing in a blind frenzy.

Bowbreaker slipped away from a punch from the abomination's spike. His counterattack bit deep into the monsters elbow, causing it to dangle from the limb.

Queen Esmarelda hit the arm of her chair with her fist. "No! This can't be happening! I want to see them die!"

The mob's loyalty started to sway in a new direction. Before, they wanted Bowbreaker's blood, but they began to shout for victory.

"Bowbreaker! Bowbreaker! Bowbreaker!"

Queen Esmarelda's face turned bloodred. She glared at Commander Roddley and said, "Do your duty and silence them!"

The abomination reeled, but it was far from over. It shrugged off each attack and came back harder with whatever it had left.

Bowbreaker slipped on a piece of the monster's flesh forcing him to hack into the monster sideways. He fell on his back, capturing the abomination's attention. It pounced at Bowbreaker with what was left of its arms and started pounding.

A spiked fist missed Bowbreaker's face by inches. The

hulk pinned him with a knee and opened its jaws wide enough to swallow Bowbreaker's head whole. It grabbed the sword by the blade and ripped it free.

Weaponless, Bowbreaker squirmed under the monster's body. He took a punch in the belly that knocked the wind out of him. The beast pulled its spiked hand back.

The audience chanted, "Bowbreaker! Bowbreaker! Bowbreaker!"

Though the tide had turned in the stands, it hadn't in the arena. Bowbreaker's final fight was at hand. He locked eyes with the abomination.

In the woodland, he could commune with animals and settle their spirits. They befriended him.

The abomination, however, was no animal. It was a creation of the abyss, fused together with dark magic and hate. Its beady eyes simmered with hunger. Globs of warm saliva dripped from its mouth. It was death incarnate. It lived for one reason: to devour.

Yet it paused.

Adana struck from its blind spot. Her sword blade bit into the corner of its eye.

It reared, back straightening, and flung its four arms wide.

Adana ducked, but the bottom arm hit her, knocking her backward and sending her sprawling across the dirt.

Bowbreaker gasped for breath. He'd spotted something.

Beneath the abomination's arms were gills that waved like they were in the sea.

He crawled and tumbled away from the abomination, but it snatched his leg and dragged him back.

He spotted the dagger that had fallen from Adana's grip. Stretching, he grabbed it.

The abomination covered him like a blanket, trapping him. Its frame blotted out the sky.

Covered in darkness, Bowbreaker twisted from the monster's grip and stabbed into the creature's soft fins. He hit a sweet spot, and his hand sank into the flesh.

The abomination grabbed a handful of hair and pulled as it shrieked.

Bowbreaker felt a heartbeat in his hand. He shoved his arm in, down to the elbow. The dagger struck meat.

The heart inside the massive body thumped once then beat no more.

The creature collapsed, crushing Bowbreaker. His strength was sapped, and his arm was trapped. He couldn't move and fought for breath, but it wouldn't come. Drained of all vitality, he started to suffocate and black out.

21

Strong hands grabbed Bowbreaker's arm and pulled him from under the abomination's body. He gasped for breath, and his eyes fluttered open.

Adana peered down at him. "Are you going to lie there all day, brother? Or are you waiting for me to sing your favorite lullaby?"

Sheela and Raghan strained to lift the abomination off him.

"Will you pull him all the way out? My back is breaking," Raghan said.

Bowbreaker crawled the rest of the way out, and Sheela and Raghan let the monster down with a groan.

"Whew! That thing stinks," Sheela said as she fanned her nose.

Shouts and the rattling of metal caught Bowbreaker's

attention. He raised his gaze to the stands, fully expecting to see the Golden Sentries with their range weapons pointed at him. But he was wrong.

"What is this?" he asked.

"Your people are rioting," Adana said with a grin.

The audience had come to life and swarmed the Golden Sentries and Black Guards. Three elves in woodsman cloaks dashed down the steps and tackled a Golden Sentry. They knocked the soldier over the walls and onto the iron rods.

"Is this what I think it is?" Bowbreaker asked, his voice filled with passion.

"Aye, brother. This is the revolution you've been waiting for," Adana replied.

For the first time in a long time, he huffed a laugh. "You had this planned all along, didn't you? And you didn't tell me?"

"Why ruin the surprise? After all, it's nearly impossible to catch you off guard." Adana pumped her sword in the air and shouted, "For Bowbreaker!"

Armed elven warriors poured through the tunnels and emerged into the stands. They took the Golden Sentries and Black Guard by storm.

Innocent bystanders fled, but others, caught up in the skirmish, took up arms from fallen soldiers and began to fight.

Elven allies spotted their leader and shouted at him

with their weapons raised high. "Bowbreaker! Bowbreaker!"

The clamor of battle became louder and more violent. The queen's soldiers were no push-overs and the best trained in the land. Golden Sentries fought against the tide with lethal precision. Elven blood from both east and west of the Great River was spilled.

Adana walked over to Archbow, and Bowbreaker joined her. The stalwart elf was dead. A tear ran down Adana's cheek.

"He was your betrothed, wasn't he?" Bowbreaker asked.

She nodded. "Yes. But he always said he would gladly give his life for me. For his friends. For all in need." She kissed Archbow's cheek. "You would have liked him. And he admired you as well."

He hugged his sister. "I'm sorry."

Raghan started shouting at their allies. "The queen! Get the queen! She's escaping!"

A group of elves in the midst of the upheaval noticed the queen and a host of her men making a break for the tunnels. The queen's marksmen guarded Esmarelda, firing their bows with lethal accuracy and dropping elves with shot after shot. They were getting away.

"I need a bow," Bowbreaker said as he charged toward the wall, waving his arms.

Queen Esmarelda made her way through the stands, hiking her chain-mail dress up. Commander Roddley carried the train. She stumbled and fell, and he helped her up.

She kicked him and screamed, "Get this ridiculous thing off me!"

A young elf slipped through the battle, carrying a bow and quiver. He made it to the arena wall and tossed them to Bowbreaker.

From behind, a Black Guard stuck the young man and shoved the already-dead elf over the wall.

Bowbreaker snatched up the bow and grabbed an arrow. In the flick of a snake's tongue, he shot the Black Guard through the throat. The man fell backward, dying.

After shouldering the quiver, Bowbreaker nocked another arrow and spotted the queen. Their eyes met.

With a crazed look in her eyes, she pointed at him and said, "Marksmen! Slay him!"

Bowbreaker fired the first shot before the marksmen had even spotted him. His arrow planted inside an elf's heart.

Marksmen. Ha. I'll show them what a marksman is.

He loaded and fired arrow number two as the enemies stretched their bowstrings back. The arrow whistled through the air and struck a marksman in the breast plate. By the time the arrow hit, he'd nocked another and pulled back.

The third marksman fired.

Bowbreaker leaned away as the arrow whistled by, then he let his arrow fly.

The last marksman died with an arrow sticking out of the front of his skull.

Queen Esmarelda's mouth hung open.

"Go, my queen. Go!" Commander Roddley urged her.

They scrambled away, and Bowbreaker let three more arrows fly, one right after the other. *Thuk! Thuk! Thuk!*

Commander Roddley's back arched. Three arrows were stuck in his ribs. He dropped his sword and tumbled over the benches.

The elves leading the revolt had blocked all the exits. Queen Esmarelda had nowhere to go. As the enemy closed in, she backed down the steps, climbed over the wall, and jumped into the arena. "Guh!"

"What's she doing?" Adana asked.

"Want me to kill her?" Raghan aimed his spear. "I'll do it."

"No, wait," Bowbreaker said as he lowered his bow.

Dragging her chain-mail dress behind her, Queen Esmarelda limped toward him. "You cannot win, Bowbreaker. This is not possible." She sobbed. "You must spare me."

"Look around you, Esmarelda. The elves have awakened. You and your allies have lost," he said.

"You're right." She stumbled aimlessly toward the

abomination. "Look what you've done. You defeated that which no elf has killed."

Raghan cleared his throat and said, "He had some help."

The queen dropped to her knees. "Please, Bowbreaker, forgive me. I will be your servant if you spare me."

He approached her and said, "I'll let the people decide what is to be done with you. But I have a feeling that keeping you alive is dangerous. I believe they'll feel so too."

She dropped her head and started crying. "But I loved you. That's all I ever did."

"I wish I could believe that." He came closer. "Regardless, justice must be served if we're to heal our nation."

Queen Esmarelda peered at him with sad eyes. "Yes, you're right. Justice must be served. But not before my revenge!"

"Look out!" Adana cried.

The queen lunged with a dagger she'd concealed. She aimed for Bowbreaker's heart and struck like a cat.

He grabbed her wrist with one hand, pulled her up to the tips of her toes, and glared into her eyes, squeezing until the dagger fell from her fingers. "Your lies have finally caught up with you. It's over, Esmarelda."

She spit in his face. "I hate you."

He shoved her toward the abomination and said, "You hate everything. Sheela, find some shackles and secure her."

Rahdeen the Abomination spasmed. Its jaws opened wide, and it struck out and clamped down on the queen, killing her instantly.

Alarmed, Adana said, "It lives!"

"No," Bowbreaker replied. "That was its death throes."

"You knew that was going to happen, didn't you?"

Bowbreaker shrugged. "I only suspected."

The Golden Sentries and Black Guard had thrown down their arms and surrendered.

The people had spoken and were shouting victory. "Bowbreaker! Bowbreaker! Bowbreaker!"

NALZAMBOR

GREY CLOAK, Dyphestive, and Zora approached the farming establishment from the east, following a muddy trail that snaked through the hilly paths down into the valley.

As they approached the small town, at least a score of men came toward them. They wore pieces of armor in poor condition. Their weapons, short swords and axes, were notched and rusty. Hair hung over their eyes, and many of them were barefoot.

"Easy," Grey Cloak said in a friendly voice. "We're only seeking some direction."

"Look at them. They're thieves," one of the men said. He was a small, squat fellow carrying a butcher knife. "We don't have any food left for you Raiders. You took it all the last time."

"We aren't raiding anything," Grey Cloak answered. He kept his hands up and smiled. "All we want to know is where in Nalzambor we are. That's all we're asking."

"Don't answer him. It's a trick," the squat man said to the biggest man in the group. "What sort of man doesn't know where he is?"

The leader, well past his prime, stroked the curls of his gray beard with one hand and held a long sword in decent condition in the other. "They don't look like Raiders. Them two is elves, by the looks of them." He raised his chin. "What are you looking for?"

"Dragon Home," Grey Cloak replied.

"See? He speaks madness, Jordun. Dragon Home is gone a thousand years," the rotund man said.

"Take it easy, Hurley. There ain't no harm in giving them directions." Jordun gave them a long, hard look, particularly at Zora and her satchel. He made a sucking sound and spit out tobacco juice. "You're northwest of Dragon Home. A fair distance. But you can't miss it." He spit again. "Or what is left of it."

"Is the walk long?" Dyphestive asked.

The men grumbled, and some of them laughed.

"You don't have much choice but to walk. Ain't no horses left around here," Jordun said.

His men sniggered.

"But you can't miss the Mountain of Doom, as we call it." Jordun pointed southeast toward the hills. "You're south of the lake below the settlement. You need to head back over the hills and keep going south. However, on foot, it will take days, and there are many dangers."

Grey Cloak nodded and said, "Thank you. We'll be on our way, Jordun."

Jordun jerked his head to one side, and the militia spread out and circled Grey Cloak, Dyphestive, and Zora.

"Now, hold on there." He pointed a finger at Grey Cloak. "We helped you. It's only proper that you help us."

Zora bristled. "For giving us directions? Let's go. They're nothing but backwoods highwaymen."

"We didn't come here to spill blood, Jordun," Grey Cloak warned him. "I suggest you have your men back off. You don't know what you're dealing with."

Hurley moved to Jordun's side and said, "Listen to him. He threatens us."

"Easy, Hurley. Let me do the talking." He sucked his teeth and spit. "I'll tell you what, stranger. Let me have the satchel the lady is carrying, and we'll let you go in peace."

Zora moved the satchel to her back and said, "I'd like to see you take it."

"Oh, I'm not going to do it," Jordun replied. "I'll have our guardian do that." He gave a sharp whistle.

Hurley teetered back and forth. "You're going to wish you'd never tried to cross us. No one invades our border without having to pay. Raider or not."

From behind the group, a moose of a man lumbered

down the dirt road. He was joined by two more brutes of a similar ilk. All three of them were bigger than Dyphestive, and they appeared to have a lot of ogre blood in them. They carried wooden clubs with metal spikes driven through the heads.

Hurley stuck his chest out and smacked the flat of his butcher knife against his hand.

The trio of brutes glowered cockily at Grey Cloak, Dyphestive, and Zora.

Jordun's smile was a mouthful of tobacco-stained teeth. "I'll take that satchel now." He leered at Zora. "That and everything else I desire."

23

Grey Cloak didn't waste any time. He unloaded a string of energy from the Rod of Weapons, which lit up one half ogre like a burning firefly.

Dyphestive stuck his sword into the ground and charged the next nearest ogre. It brought down its club but not before Dyphestive punched it in the gut and knocked the wind from the brute.

Whirling around, Dyphestive caught the last ogre midattack. He lifted the beastly man like a child and drove him headfirst into the ground

In moments, all three ogres were on the ground, knocked out or gasping for breath. The majority of the militia fled.

Jordun found himself in a precarious predicament. Zora hip tossed him to the ground and held a dagger against his throat. "What was it you said you wanted from me?"

Jordun swallowed. The lump in his throat rolled underneath the blade, nicking his skin. Sweating and with a feverish look in his eyes, he said, "N-Nothing. Nothing at all, miss. I'm happy to help. Ask me anything. I'd be obliged to answer."

"I don't recall you offering the same courtesy earlier. Why is that?"

The militia leader shrugged. "Sometimes I'm a bad judge of character. Ask Hurley."

Hurley was sprinting toward the town. He kept falling down, looking back, fighting his way to his feet, and running again.

"I don't think Hurley's going to vouch for you." Zora took her knife away from his neck and pushed off his chest with her knee. Then she gave him a swift kick in the ribs.

Jordun groaned.

"Easy, Zora," Grey Cloak said as he spun the rod around his body. "I wouldn't want our friends to think we're harsh people. You'll give us a bad reputation."

"I ruined my reputation when I started spending time with you."

He smirked. "Funny. I always thought it was the other way around. After all, you did relieve me of my dagger."

Zora rolled her eyes. "Oh, so this is all my fault."

"I sleep better if I think of it that way."

Dyphestive was helping the half ogre he'd punched to his knees.

"What are you doing?" Grey Cloak asked. "Playing good brute, bad brute?"

"I hit him pretty hard. I wanted to make sure he wasn't going to die. He might have a family," Dyphestive said and gave his attacker a worried look.

Grey Cloak shook his head. "I really don't understand him. Do you?" he asked Zora.

She shrugged. "He was always nicer than both of us."

"I think he's going to be fine." Dyphestive patted the half ogre on the shoulders, walked away, pulled the Iron Sword free of the dirt, and joined his friends. "Southeast, is it?"

"Aye," Grey Cloak stated.

Jordun sat up and said, "Friends, you have shown desperate, greedy men mercy today. I hope it bodes you well. But I warn you. The Raiders rule the land. They are a force of reckoning. I'd do my best to avoid them if I could. They aren't simple men such as us. They are truly merciless."

"Thanks for sharing," Zora said. "As if you have any credibility."

The half ogre stood and said, "He speaks truth." He nodded at Dyphestive. "Be wary." He pointed at a nearby stretch of road. "Follow that road. And if you hear a skreeling sound, hide."

Dyphestive nodded back. "We will take that under advisement."

They moved down the road.

"It's a good thing Anya wasn't here," Zora said with one final glance back. "Or they'd all be dead."

Grey Cloak and Dyphestive chuckled.

"Speaking of Anya, I hope she and Streak haven't run into any misfortune like we did," Grey Cloak said.

"How are they going to find us if we keep moving?" Zora asked.

"Don't worry. Streak can find me. That's never a problem for him." He used his rod like a walking stick. "I wonder what's going to be so fearsome about the Raiders. I don't recall Nath mentioning them. Did he say anything to you, Dyphestive?"

Dyphestive raised his shoulders. "No."

"Well," Grey Cloak continued, "hopefully Anya will find them first."

Anya and Streak traveled about a thousand feet above a bleak and barren land. The forest hills were brown with rare patches of green. Ponds and streams were dried up.

"This is a wasteland," Anya said as she leaned over the saddle, looking for any sign of life. "It sickens me to think that Black Frost is feasting on this world."

Streak nodded. "Yeah, no one should be that hungry. Do you see that?"

Smoke was coming from campfires below, with hundreds of people clustering around them.

"It appears to be a settlement of some sort."

"Perhaps they'll know what we're looking for," Streak said. "Maybe we should fly down there and you can ask them. After all, you're really great with people."

"Funny. Perhaps I'll offer them a dragon sacrifice."

"Oh, you're cold. I'll give you that." Streak's eyes widened. "But I don't think either of us will need to pay them a visit."

"Why is that?"

"Take a closer look."

Creatures launched from the ground and took to the sky, making a beeline straight toward Anya and Streak.

A chill raced down Anya's spine. "What are those things?"

"I don't know, but they are ten shades of ugly." He picked up speed. "And I don't think we want it rubbing off on us either."

24

———

Five dragons pursued Streak and Anya. They were the size of middling dragons, hornless, and had black scales on their faces that matched their wings. Gray scales covered most of their bodies.

An orc-like man was the lone rider. He wore a metal skullcap with two horns and a full suit of studded-leather armor. He pointed at Anya and shouted orders.

The gray dragons picked up speed and bore down on Streak.

"They're gaining," Anya warned him.

"Let them try. They won't catch me." Streak turned his head around, his hairless, scaly eyebrows raised. "They're pretty fast, though, or have you gained weight?"

Anya kicked her heels into his ribs. "Watch it."

"I was only kidding."

She yanked on the reins. "No, watch it!"

Five more dragons dropped from the cover of the clouds and dove across Streak's path.

He veered right and barrel-rolled through the sky then pumped his wings and picked up speed.

"Where did they come from?" he asked.

"I don't know, but we need to get away. Stretch the distance. We might be in their territory, and they're defending it."

"Defending what? There's nothing down there but fallen trees and dirt."

"I don't know, but do you want to slow down so we can ask them?"

"Ha. Your dry humor is growing on me. I knew you had it in you."

Anya kept her attention on the dragons. There were ten, and they were led by two dragon riders shouting and pounding their chests. Blood was in their eyes. She had the sinking feeling they wouldn't rest.

They traveled at least a couple of leagues, but their pursuers didn't abandon the hunt. If anything, they picked up speed.

"Are you flying your fastest?" she asked.

"No. I'm saving energy. Once they start to fade, I'll make a break for it."

Anya shook her head. Getting away from their pursuers

was one thing, but they were also going to be blocked off from returning to Grey Cloak and the others.

"We need to turn back," she said.

"What? Why?"

"Because the others are behind us, and we can't be separated."

"I say we lose them and come back for them later."

"No, they'll be waiting." She drew her sword and buckled her helmet's chinstrap. "We need to act now."

"If you say so. I'm bigger than they are. Perhaps that will scare them," Streak said. "As for you, you're just scary." He turned his wings and shot straight for the clouds.

Anya held the reins tightly and squeezed the saddle with her thighs.

Streak looped upside down in the air. Several dragons jetted under them. Others tried to follow, but they couldn't pull off the same maneuver, and a pair of them crashed into each other as they tried to turn in the air.

Streak dropped behind the thunder of dragons.

They shrieked as they looked back.

"I don't know what you have in mind, but you do what you need to do, and I'll do what I can," he said as he sped closer to the group.

Anya was in a new world, but her energy tingled all over. She tapped into her wizardry, and her eyes became like fire.

One of the dragon riders turned around, and the whites of his eyes showed he'd seen her face.

"Looking for me?" she shouted.

A thunderclap sounded, and lightning flashed.

The lead dragon rider's jaw dropped.

Lightning struck one of the dragons closest to him, blowing the wings from its body and sending it plummeting toward the ground in a stream of smoke.

"Great shot!" Streak said. He caught up to the dragon in the rear, bit its tail, and yanked.

The dragon made an awful *skree*. It bucked, struggling to break free.

Streak's chest expanded, and flames spewed from his nostrils, then he opened his jaws and unleashed more.

Fire struck two dragons in their backs. One lost a tail, and the other's wings caught fire. Both of them shrieked.

"That sounds awful," Streak said as he flew through a cloud of smoke he'd made. "You might want to have a doctor look at that."

The eight remaining dragons veered away.

Anya spotted the shock and fear in the orcen men's eyes. They weren't ready for a fight and fled for the clouds.

"It looks like they don't want any part of this," Streak said. "Do you want me to stop chasing them?"

"Keep after them. I want to make sure they don't turn back," she replied as she sheathed her sword. "But I don't think you're right."

The dragon riders flung something over their heads, and two balls of energy hung in the sky.

"What's that?" Streak asked.

"I don't know. Go around it."

Both balls exploded in a bright flash of blinding light.

"I can't see!" Streak said.

Anya saw a field of black and blurry colors. Her stomach twisted into knots. The wind whistling through her ears slowed. "It's a trap! Turn around."

"Turn around where? I can't see anything!"

They were completely disoriented.

A great net dropped over both her and Streak like a blanket. By the time her vision cleared, they were trapped, and the dragons were towing them through the sky.

How did they do that? Who are these people?

DARK MOUNTAIN

GOSSAMER TRAILED behind Datris as they traversed the one hundred flights of stairs outside of Black Frost's temple, through the icy wind.

His foot slipped for the third time. His thighs burned, and he'd lost all feeling in his toes and hands.

Panting, Gossamer said, "A moment, Datris. I need to rest."

Datris stopped on the next landing. His hands were tucked inside his white robes, and his breath frosted when he spoke. "I'll be glad to. I can't feel my ears, and my legs are aching. I'm not in the same condition I was not so long ago." He leaned over the edge and stared at the jagged clumps of black rock. "I've become soft. The temple climb makes me queasy."

Gossamer climbed up to the landing and joined Datris. "Are you certain there isn't another way inside?"

"Nothing I'm aware of. Black Frost built his temple like a fortress. There is only one way inside," Datris answered. His teeth chattered. He looked at his fingers and flexed them. "Can you feel your fingers? Mine will move, but I don't feel them."

Gossamer breathed into his hands. "We'd better keep moving, or we might freeze before we make it to the top."

"Agreed. Would you like to lead the way?"

A brisk wind blew Gossamer's hair in his eyes. He brushed it aside and said, "Why not. We're over halfway there, and I might need you to stop me if I fall and slide down these stairs."

"I won't let that happen," Datris assured him.

"Well, it might be a better fate than facing Black Frost. I hope we can fool him."

"Don't think about it and let me do the talking. If he doesn't address you, don't speak. All we need to do is go back down inside. Our mission will be safe then."

Gossamer nodded and resumed the agonizing trek. In his lifetime, he'd given the weather little thought, but recently, he'd come to a conclusion. *If I survive this, I will always live where it's warm.*

Snowflakes stung his face, but he blocked out the pain and focused on their mission. It would take strong magic to release Zanna Paydark from her stone form and switch her with Datris. She and Datris had to resume each other's bodies as well. Gossamer had everything he needed and the spells in mind. All they had to do was pull it off without tipping off Black Frost and his minions. It sounded easy, but impossible was more likely.

They climbed up the last flight of stairs. Gasping, they reached the platform and bent over with their hands on their knees.

Nothing had changed since Gossamer's last visit. Black Frost's gargantuan body filled the temple's platform, towering over them by several stories. The black claws on his back legs were bigger than a man. Each ebony scale shone like snake skin and was as big as a soldier's buckler.

Dragon guardians were perched on the rim of the temple, facing outward. Grand dragons made up part of the host, anchoring the corners and the middle, with scores of middling dragons in between.

Gossamer had a sinking feeling as he followed Datris across the temple's flat roof. Black Frost's vast army would be impossible to defeat in a conventional way. Simply put, he had too much dragon power, not to mention that he was as big as a town or small city.

He caught up with Datris, who made his way alongside Black Frost's front paw.

Datris stopped, turned his head, and gave Gossamer a nod of assurance.

As Gossamer spied the majestic set of horns on Black Frost's head, he followed his friend to face the dragon.

Black Frost's head lay flat on the roof. His blue eyes, bigger than full-length mirrors, were opened wide. They burned with a blue flame.

Hot air eased out of Black Frost's mouth, through his sharp, pearly white teeth, instantly warming Gossamer from head to toe.

They waited.

The pupils in Black Frost's eyes grew, and one side of his mouth curled up. "Ah, my servants have returned after all this time." He raised his massive head a few feet off the ground. "I've missed my tiny companions. I take it you have news that will please me?"

Datris bowed. "Yes, Majestic One. I, too, have missed being directly in your service. We have come to report that the Time Mural has been fully rebuilt, as you commanded. It is fully operational."

The rims around Black Frost's eyes widened. His steady gaze fell upon Gossamer. "Have you anything to report, my servant?"

Gossamer bowed. "It is as Datris stated. The Time Mural is operational."

Black Frost yawned. His open mouth created a cavern vast enough for a family of dragons to live in. His breath reeked of sulfur and brimstone. Deep within, a fire glowed, and heat seeped out.

Gossamer stepped back as Black Frost's jaws closed.

"If that is true, tell me how you know it works," Black Frost said.

Datris nodded. "As you wish, Your Grandness."

"I don't want to hear it from you, Datris." He shifted his gaze to Gossamer. "I want to hear it from him."

26

GOSSAMER CLEARED HIS DRY THROAT. The last thing he wanted to do was talk. He hated lying, but he'd been living a lie for a decade, running an impossible deception through thick and thin. He caught his breath and clamped a hand over his trembling fingers.

So long as I tell the truth, he won't suspect any different. You can do this.

"Great One, with confidence, I can tell you that I have experienced the advantages of the Time Mural firsthand. I have traveled to another world and back again."

Black Frost gave him an approving look. "Do tell, Gossamer. I wish to know more about another world I can devour. Is it as succulent as the one I feast on now?"

"Bish is a barren world, with cities rotting in the sand. The people are spirited and lively but the land, as dry as the bones of the dead." He took a breath. "I saw very little, aside from one city and the harsh climate."

"Did they use magic?"

"Indeed, they did. Their craft is similar to Gapoli's. I felt it running through my skin and bones, but I had little reason to use my own. Revealing my powers would be dangerous."

Black Frost nodded. Smoke huffed out of his nostrils and drifted toward the clouds.

"I take it you went to this world to find Dirklen and Magnolia, did you not?" The great dragon tilted his head. "And they have returned with you?" he asked.

"No, my lord. Though I found them, they were prisoners. I was unable to free them. They'd committed many crimes against Bish's people. They were under a death sentence." He swallowed. "With greater mastery of the Time Mural, it is possible for another trip back. But when I was summoned back, I missed any opportunity I had. It is whatever Your Majesty wishes."

Gossamer hadn't lied, but he hadn't revealed the full picture of the circumstances either.

Black Frost's sigh stirred Gossamer's hair and clothing. "You've done well, Gossamer and Datris. You have served and shown courage, venturing into the unknown. Perhaps you can send Honzur and Commander Covis on a return trip to Bish for further exploration."

"I'd like that," Gossamer said. He hated them both, even

though they were gone. It was best to show his selfish ambition to Black Frost, making his story all the more believable. He bowed. "Pardon, my lord. I should not speak ill of your servants."

"I have plenty of servants, as you can see. My dragons are the dearest by far. I care little for the men of the world who kiss my scales. They are only one means to an end and serve their purpose. But I do appreciate a faithful effort. Is there anything you require of me?"

Datris dropped to his knees and bowed. "No, Great One. We live to serve."

Gossamer joined his friend on his knees. "We only wish to prepare another portal for you, the same as the one that strengthens you now."

"Then do it, worms. And do it with haste. As one world dies, I crave another."

The elves bowed, stood, and bowed again.

"As you wish, Majestic Master," Datris said. "We shall do as you please immediately."

Without another word, they hurried away, found the entrance into the bowels of the temple, took the steps down, and didn't stop until they reached the bottom.

Gossamer braced his back against the wall and caught his breath. His heart raced. "I can't believe we made it this far," he muttered.

Datris put a finger to his lips. "The less we speak, the

better." He nodded at the nearest corridor. "Let's go and quickly."

Gossamer took a moment to observe his impressive surroundings.

The temple's core was hollow, and thick, huge stones made up the walls. The support columns were massive. Running along the walls were streams of energy that fed the platform on the top, where Black Frost absorbed more power. The glint in the streams was not as vibrant as the last time he'd studied it. The brightness had weakened.

Nalzambor has little time left, if any life remains at all. But what will happen to Black Frost if he cannot feed? Will he shrink?

He hurried after Datris, who had waved him on.

"We need to make haste, as Black Frost stated. Not that I'm in any hurry." Datris led the way into the chamber where the statues of Dyphestive's father, Olgstern Strong-hair, and Grey Cloak's mother, Zanna Paydark, were facing another Time Mural. He let out a long breath. "This is it."

"Are you certain you want to do this?" Gossamer asked.

Datris nodded as he stared at Zanna. "I feel this is my purpose. It is the moment I've been waiting for." He touched her limbs. "If she doesn't go back in time and find her son, it will end for all of us—as well as other worlds."

Gossamer peeked into the hall. No one approached, and he hadn't seen anyone since they entered the temple. "Then we'd better be quick about it." He took Datris by the hand and held on to the statue. "I hope she's quick to understand once she is free."

"She will be," Datris assured him. "Do it."

Gossamer closed his eyes. His thoughts sank into a world of magic, and he drew forth great power unlike any he'd summoned before.

Zanna Paydark's hard body turned into flesh. She blinked and opened her eyes wide. Then she placed daggers against Gossamer's and Datris's throats. "Who are you? What is the meaning of this?"

27

IT TOOK SOME FAST TALKING, but Zanna finally lowered her daggers.

Gossamer rubbed his neck. "I know everything I told you is difficult to believe, but it's the only way. I can tell you more, but time is pressing, and we need to depart immediately."

Zanna spun her daggers and stuffed them into her sheaths. She indicated Olgstern Stronghair's statue. "What about him?"

"He's not part of the plan yet, but he will soon be free as well," Gossamer replied.

"I believe you. And I'm curious to see what has become of my son for the last twenty seasons."

"It's about ten seasons for him, but that's another story."

Her brow furrowed then eased. "I'll be looking forward to it. All right, Gossamer, do what you must do."

Gossamer's back was as tight as a bowstring, but the tension in his shoulders started to ease. He hadn't known whether Zanna would come aboard after the quick version of the outlandish tale he'd told her. He had trouble believing it himself. He took a breath and said, "Datris, assume her place."

Datris stepped onto the spot where Zanna had been standing. Sweat beaded on his brow. He asked Zanna, "How bad is it?"

"It's impossible to say. Do your best to pretend you're asleep." She squeezed Datris's hand. "You are very brave for such a young one."

"This is my purpose. It must be done. I'm honored," Datris replied.

"Hold hands," Gossamer said to them. "When I cast the spell, you will assume each other's identities. The magic is strong, and I don't know how long it will hold, but when you're turned to stone, it should be permanent." He stepped closer to Datris. "Are you ready?"

"Yes."

Gossamer seized both of them by the wrist, above the spot where they held hands. He closed his eyes and summoned his wizardry. Energy swelled inside him as he let the enchanted words release from his lips as fast as hummingbird wings.

Power flowed from his chest to his fingertips. Warm, raw vivacity spread into his comrades. Three became one. The essence of each crossed through him into the other. He felt their thoughts. A compelling source of goodness was in both of them.

Then the warmth passed, and the air cooled. His knees buckled, and he swayed.

Strong hands held him up and wiped his damp locks from his face. He opened his eyes.

Zanna's stone statue was back in place.

He studied Datris's face. "Did it work?"

"I am Zanna but trapped in this boyish form. Hmm. I sound like him too." She smirked. "That might take some getting used to."

"Remember, you are him, and he is you." Gossamer glanced at the statue. "I believe you have the better end of the deal."

"Trust me. I am, but we shall free that young man." She grabbed Olgstern's wrist. "We will free both of them."

Gossamer couldn't help but ask, "What happened? You were close, weren't you?"

"To destroying the portal?" She nodded. "Yes, we were close, but Black Frost knew it would come, and we weren't careful enough. Too eager, one might say."

As they abandoned the chamber and headed up the stairs, she continued, "Olgstern and I sniffed out the Day of Betrayal. The last of the Sky Riders faced off against Black

Frost's army of Riskers. We attacked Dark Mountain, but it was more or less a decoy."

She stopped and rubbed her thighs. "Goy. My thighs are burning. It's been quite some time since I walked." She looked up and down the stairwell of the vast chamber. "We rode a dragon down and didn't figure we'd have the chance to climb back up." She began moving again. "Anyway, we knew the source of Black Frost's power fed him from the belly of the temple. We had spies, and my husband, Jerrik Paydark, was one of those in connection with those who created the portal."

"What happened to them?"

"Once Black Frost began feeding, he killed them all. Jerrik realized his mistake. He tried to put an end to Black Frost's plan and close the portal. He warned me of the trap and what was happening." Her chin dipped. "He was gone before I could rescue him. It was too late.

"Olgstern and I knew what to look for. When the war between the Sky Riders and Riskers began on the Day of Betrayal, we slipped through their defenses undetected. We battled through some meager defenses of the nearly abandoned temple, and once we discovered the archway to the portal, Olgstern hoped to batter it down using his great strength."

"Wouldn't that have killed you?" Gossamer asked.

"As I said, we didn't plan to climb these steps. But Black Frost, as mighty as he is, was no fool. The crafty serpent plans two steps ahead. We overcame one trap in the temple only to completely overlook the other. I should have detected the floor plates in the archway chamber. I missed, and the moment we went to take down the archway, we turned to stone."

They came to the top of the stairs. Before they moved to the top of the temple, Gossamer stopped her. "Once you head out, keep going. Black Frost knows we will take our leave."

She nodded, and they emerged on the platform and stood in the icy winds of the north.

Gossamer led the way to the outer stairs.

Black Frost groaned. His low voice shook the roof. "Datris, come."

Zanna froze and said to Gossamer, "I can handle this."

He waited as she moved out of sight for a face-to-face with Black Frost.

Lords of the Sky, he is enormous.

Zanna tried not to marvel, but Black Frost had grown at least five times his previous size since the last time she'd seen him, and he was huge before. She moved along his front paw, stood before him, and bowed. "What is it, Grand One? How may I serve you?" she asked.

Black Frost eyed her and said, "Your trip into the temple

was quick. Did you find everything you need to make the proper preparations?"

"We are well suited to do what needs to be done," she replied.

He nodded. "Tell me—can you do this without Gossamer?"

"In time, but the wizardry is not my craft. But I will do what pleases my lord when the time comes."

"I know you will. Well, Datris, I am eager for the next step. My hunger grows. Take one of my dragons to the Wizard Watch. Use the one closest. It is fully operational, is it not?"

She nodded. "We control them all."

"Good. Now, begone." Black Frost closed his eyes. "But I want results, and I want them soon."

"As you wish," she said and quickly departed.

A grand dragon dropped from the sky and landed on the roof.

She waved Gossamer over. "Get on."

"We're flying?"

"We don't fly." She took the front seat of the saddle. "We ride the sky!"

NALZAMBOR

A SINKING feeling formed in the pit of Grey Cloak's stomach. He stopped on a rocky rise that overlooked the next stretch of barren land.

"Something's wrong," he said.

Dyphestive joined him and narrowed his eyes. "What? I don't see anything but brittle trees and dirt."

"It's not that. It's Streak. He's in danger."

"How do you know?"

"Oh, I know." Grey Cloak moved forward, picking up speed.

Zora stayed on his tail, and Dyphestive did the best he could to keep up.

The sun had begun to set behind the distant hills. They ran for leagues, not stopping until Zora caught up with Grey Cloak and grabbed his wrist.

"Will you slow down? You run like a gazelle." She pinched her sides as she gasped for air. "I'm only part elf, you know." She looked back. "And we lost your brother an hour ago."

"He'll catch up. He always does. Wait for him." He took off his boots and gave them to her. "And hold these. I can run faster without them. I'll double back once I find Streak." Then he sprinted away.

Zora crinkled her nose and dropped the boots. "Ew."

Dyphestive caught up with Zora about thirty minutes later. He walked with his sword resting on one shoulder and the other arm swinging. "What happened to Grey?"

"He took off like his pants were on fire." She handed him Grey Cloak's boots. "He wanted you to hold on to these for him."

Dyphestive huffed. "Sure he did." He tucked the boots under his arm. "All right, let's follow his dust."

"After you."

"No, after you."

Zora shrugged. She was a decent tracker, and her elven vision helped in the darkness. Besides, Grey Cloak wasn't trying to be discreet. She had no trouble following him at first.

She stopped and took a knee. Placing a hand on the ground she said, "His footprints are gone."

Dyphestive peered down then checked the skies. "Do you think something caught him?"

"I didn't see or hear anything."

"Let's keep going in the direction we were going. We're bound to pick him up somewhere else, I'd imagine."

"Strange," she said as she resumed her walk.

They marched for a long time under the dark and cloudy sky.

Dyphestive clamped a hand over her shoulder and pulled her down. "Someone's coming."

A silhouette approached in the darkness, waving their arms. "It's me. Grey."

Zora popped up. "Thank goodness. Your tracks vanished. We thought someone had snatched you."

When Grey Cloak smiled, his white teeth showed. "I can thank the Cloak of Legends for that. It does a fine job hiding my passage." He sighed. "But I fear I have bad news."

"What?" Zora and Dyphestive asked in unison.

"Streak and Anya have been captured."

"By whom?" Zora asked.

"I think it's the Raiders Jordun mentioned. They have a settlement not far from here. I came back to warn you before you stumbled upon them."

Dyphestive tossed Grey Cloak his boots. He gripped the Iron Sword with both hands and asked, "How many?"

"A lot."

"I can handle a lot."

Still standing, Grey Cloak pulled his boots on. "I'm sure you can, but this mission is one of discretion. I don't want to wage a war if we don't have to." He stomped his foot. "Come on. I'll show you."

They moved into the hills and hid in a spot on the ridge that overlooked the enemy's encampment.

Hundreds of tents both large and small were spread out over a half a league. Campfires burned throughout the settlement, and warriors roamed through the night, eating and drinking.

Kneeling, Zora said, "I don't see Streak or Anya. How do you know they're in there? It's too dark to see."

"I can feel it," Grey Cloak said. He pulled his hood over his head. "I'm going to go down there and find out exactly where they are."

She grabbed his arm. "No. It's too dangerous. You'll be seen." She lifted the Scarf of Shadows and pulled it over her nose. As she vanished, she said, "I'll handle it."

"Zora, come back here," Grey Cloak said. "You can't run off like that."

"Ha ha," she said from a distance. "How does it feel?"

29

DYPHESTIVE LAY DOWN, propped himself up on one elbow, and overlooking the encampment, he said, "You care about Zora, don't you?"

"What are you talking about?"

"I can see it in your eyes. You're worried about her."

Grey Cloak eased back from the ridge. "Of course I care about her. I care about all of us."

"But her more than most, right?"

"What are you trying to do? Pay me back for teasing you?" Grey Cloak was down on one knee, but his eyes didn't leave the camp. "Yes, I think we both know that I'm fond of her, but she's fonder of Stone Face the elf."

"Ah, Bowbreaker. I wonder how he's faring."

"Well, if he's in the middle of a staring contest, I'm certain he's doing well. And what brought this up anyway?"

Dyphestive shrugged. "I don't know. But the two of you together, well, it's a good fit."

Grey Cloak had often mused about Zora and him being together, but for the most part, he had little time to think about it. He did care deeply for her, but he never really felt it was in the cards either. If something was meant to be, it would have happened already.

"Do you really think we're a good pair?" he asked.

"Like I said, you go well together. Once we see this through, I think you'd better make your move."

"What do you mean? I'm not going to settle down and start a family. I still want to do what I want to do, like when we started out. Don't you?"

"I'm not sure what's left. We've been from one side of Gapoli to the other. Now we're in another world. What else is there?"

"Huh. I never thought about it that way. Still, it would be fun to roam the territories without bloodthirsty hunters on our tails."

"But don't you think it would be more fun with her at your side?"

Grey Cloak picked a patch of dry grass from the ground. "You're being silly. And what are your plans for when we escape this madness?"

"I hadn't really thought about it. I only wanted to see how much you like Zora." Dyphestive smiled. "Now I know."

"Well, aren't you clever. I hope you're happy now."

"I was only passing the time."

Grey Cloak flung the grass at his brother. "Eat that, clever one."

Dyphestive brushed the grass out of his hair. "I'm not hungry."

The sound of wings flapping caught Grey Cloak's ears, and they both looked up.

A dragon rider holding a torch flew overhead.

"Get down," Grey Cloak said as he flattened down on the grass. Peeking out of the corner of his eye, he saw the dragon rider drop something shaped like an orb. It fell toward them then came to a stop and hovered over their position.

"What is that?" Dyphestive whispered.

The orb glowed like wildfire then exploded in a blinding flash of light. *Boomph!*

Bright spots floated in front of Grey Cloak's eyes, and his extremities tingled. He tried to stand but fell to his knees. Rubbing his eyes and tearing up, he finally blinked away the spots.

A host of orcen warriors with greenish skin had Grey Cloak and Dyphestive surrounded. They pointed crossbows and spears at their chests.

A towering brute with a metal skullcap and a stitched-up eye spoke. "Get up, intruders. Lift those hands over your heads, and get those fingers where I can see them."

He pointed at the encampment with his crossbow. "March!"

Zora stole into the camp like a ghost. Invisible, she moved on cat's feet, picking her way through the field of campfires and tents.

Warriors wandered through the settlement. Many carried jugs of wine and staggered. Others gnawed on the bones of cooked meat and sang songs in gravelly voices.

Zora pinched her nose as she squeezed between two muscular orcs.

Whew! I don't think they've ever bathed. This place is as foul as dragon dung.

She moved toward the center of the camp, where an oversize tent had guards carrying halberds outside of the entrance flap. She overheard gruff voices talking inside and took a peek.

Four soldiers in light armor were inside the room. Three of them were orcen warriors, but the fourth man stood taller than the others. His shoulders and neck swelled with muscle, and he had the head of a wolfhound. He wore a cape made of dragon scales.

"This dragon we captured is unique. Not like we've seen before. Kill it and skin it to the bone." The doglike man rapped his knuckles on a wooden table. "That dragon will fetch a high price. Our best find in years. Do as I say. So says Jumar the Gnoll. King of the Poachers. Lord of the Raiders."

The orcen soldiers nodded.

One of them said, "We will make it so. Death to the dragon. And what of the woman?"

Jumar asked, "Is she appealing?"

"I'd say for her sort."

"Then we'll make a slave out of her."

The orcs bowed, pivoted, and marched so quickly out of the room that Zora had to jump out of the way. She made a barely audible gasp.

The orcs didn't slow, but Jumar the Gnoll scanned the room. His black nose crinkled, and he sniffed and bared his teeth. The tips of his dog ears perked up higher. He slid a long dagger out of his belt and moved to the other side of the table, sniffing harder.

Zora backed away, turned toward the tent flap, and ran.

30

STREAK AND ANYA were kept inside a huge pit covered by a grid of steel. They were under heavy guard, and the soldiers who'd left Jumar's tent led Zora right to them.

She stood on the rim of the pit, staring down at her friends. Anya sat against the wall with her hands tied behind her back. Streak's mouth was bound with rope, and his wings were tied together. He was sleeping.

This isn't good at all. And here I thought I could slip in and cut some ropes, and we could fly away and be free. I should have known it would be more complicated than that. This explains why we didn't see where they were, though.

Zora sized up the warriors guarding the pit. All of them stood around the rim, facing outward, while the soldiers who'd met with Jumar discussed how they would go about killing Streak.

I can't stand around and let this happen. I need to make a distraction. That will give me time to warn Grey Cloak and Dyphestive. We're going to need their help.

The cage on top of the pit was secured by a locking bar with a pin in it. *Hmm. I'm not going to be able to lift that with these scrawny arms. But I think I can squeeze through the bars.*

She looped her satchel off her shoulder and dangled it between the bars, whispering to Anya, "Psst! Heads up!"

When she dropped the satchel, it reappeared and landed at Anya's feet. She wiggled between the bars and dropped then pulled down the Scarf of Shadows and reappeared.

Anya had a languid look in her eyes.

Zora grabbed her face and shook it. "What's wrong with you? Are you in there?"

"Zora, it's so nice of you to stop by," Anya said dreamily. "Isn't this room nice?"

"What did they do to you? How did you get captured?"

"Bright light. Bright light," Anya said like a child. She cackled. "Then they gave me water, but it made my tongue numb. But I feel warm and fuzzy inside."

"Remind me to grab some of that before we go back home. I like you like this."

"I like you too."

"Donkey skulls. This is not the Anya I need today. Is Streak drugged too?"

Anya nodded. "He drank the whole bucket." Anya slurred her next words. "He was thirsty."

"Well, they're going to kill him if we don't get him out of here."

"What? Kill him?" Anya sobbed. "Don't kill him. He's my friend."

"Zooks. This would have to happen like this." Using her dagger, Zora sliced through the cords that bound Streak's mouth and wings. His wings flopped down and covered her like a blanket, so she crawled out. Streak didn't budge an inch, and he snored.

"Say, when are you going to cut me free?" Anya asked. "My wrists are stinging, and my shoulders ache."

"Listen to me." Zora leaned Anya forward and cut her cords. "You have to snap out of it. We have to escape."

Anya shook her head. "I don't want to leave. This is my new home."

Zora slapped her hard then grabbed her by the armor and shook her like a doll. "If you don't get it together, you are going to die!"

Anya rolled her jaw. "I felt that." She giggled. "Now my face is warm like a biscuit."

"This isn't going to work." Zora sighed. "I need to get out of here. No, wait. I can use the collars to send them back. Ah-ha!" She brushed Anya's hair away from her neck. The collar was gone. "No!"

Zora spun around and looked at Streak's paw. His collar was gone too.

"Donkey skulls!" she said so loudly that she heard the scuffle of feet approaching. She covered her nose with the scarf and vanished.

An orcen warrior carrying a long spear peeked into the pit. His protruding brow knitted, then he snorted and walked away.

Zora dropped the scarf and slapped Anya again.

"Where did you go?" Anya asked.

"Never mind that. I'm going to leave. You need to, well, wake up. If you don't, you and Streak are dead."

Zora covered her face and climbed out of the cage. *I need to find those collars, and I have a feeling Jumar has them.*

The orcen soldiers were having a heated discussion about how to handle the slaughter of Streak. It sounded as if they all wanted a little something extra for themselves.

"Kill the beast first, then we shall decide," one of the orc soldiers said.

"I want a horn," another argued. He gripped a broad sword. "I'm next in line for it."

"We'll let Jumar decide," another soldier with wooly black hair running down past his neck said. "Kill first. Debate later."

A horn sounded throughout the camp, and a dragon rider flew across the sky.

The camp came to life as the people stirred.

Women and children stepped out of their tents.

A sea of Raiders shouted and parted, forming a channel between them.

Zora gasped. Grey Cloak and Dyphestive were being marched into camp in chains.

31

Zora caught Jumar coming out of his tent as the new prisoners were brought before him.

Jumar placed his hairy fists on his hips and asked, "What have we here? More spies?" He looked Dyphestive up and down. "This is a big one."

"One of our dragon riders spotted them hiding in the ridges," the leader of the orcen soldiers said. "It was a simple capture."

"So it appears." Jumar grabbed Grey Cloak by the collar. "I'll be. They wear the same raiment as the others." He got snout to nose with Grey Cloak. "Tell me, elf, what is the significance of the collar?"

"We are escaped slaves," Grey Cloak said. He gazed up at the sky. "Our masters are looking for us. We're searching for food."

Jumar scoffed. "Ha! No slave wears precious stones such as this. It's worth a fortune."

Grey Cloak shook his head. "No, they use magic to track us. The collars can kill us if they spot us. Wizards with strong magic. They will hunt us down."

"What wizards do you speak of?" Jumar picked up Grey Cloak by his clothes, lifting him off his toes. "Tell me, elf. Or I'll kill you myself!"

"Caligin," Dyphestive blurted.

Jumar dropped Grey Cloak. "What do you mean, 'Caligin'? They rule the north."

Zora didn't have any idea what the Caligin were, either, but she didn't stand around and watch Grey Cloak's charade. She stole into Jumar's tent and searched for Anya's and Streak's collars.

A strongbox sat under the table Jumar had pounded on earlier. She dragged it out and opened the lid.

The hinges groaned, so she froze and watched the tent flap. No one came. She lifted the lid all the way back and spied the twinkling gems mounted in the collars.

Whew! Finally, good fortune.

When she looped the collars over her arms, they vanished with the rest of her. She closed the lid and snuck back outside.

Jumar the dog-faced gnoll was in a heated conversation with his soldiers. Grey Cloak and Dyphestive waited, kneeling.

Zora took the opportunity to engage in a very quiet conversation with Grey Cloak. "Whatever you do, do not drink the water. It's a foul elixir. I found Anya and Streak. They are, well, drugged. The only safe thing to do is send them back."

Grey Cloak nodded. "Do what you must," he whispered.

"I can send you back too."

"No, we can handle this. Go quickly."

"Fine, but don't make this situation worse than it already is." She moved away then came back and whispered in Dyphestive's ear, "And don't you get any wild thoughts either."

Dyphestive chuckled.

The mentioning of the Caligin must have caught the Raiders off guard.

Nath had spoken about the Caligin during one of his and Dyphestive's conversations. The old hermit had spoken of many things about his world. Dyphestive hadn't thought any of them would come in handy. But one thing Nath had made perfectly clear was that the Caligin, a brood of dark elves, were to be feared.

Dyphestive leaned over and said to Grey Cloak, "Keep going with this."

"You go with it. I don't even know what a Caligin is."

"Bad elves."

"Oh." Grey Cloak perked up. "I should know a thing or two about that."

"Agreed."

"Silence!" Jumar pulled Grey Cloak up by the collar again. "The Caligin could be any elf. You, perhaps, might be one of them, trying to fool me. It might be best that I kill you—both of you—and we'll see what befalls us next."

Several dragons took to the air, led by dragon riders.

"It seems to me that you're concerned about the Caligin, and you should be. They are coming. But if you let us go, your settlement should be safe from their poison. We only want some rations, and we'll be on our way," Dyphestive said.

Jumar let go of Grey Cloak and tapped his long dagger against his chest. "Get them some *water*. Perhaps that will loosen their tongues."

As one of the Raiders hurried away, another one of the captors approached. It was the orc with an eye stitched closed. He held the Iron Sword and the Rod of Weapons. "They carried these."

Jumar's wolfish eyes widened. "Toss me that cane, Stitches," he said.

Stitches complied, and he caught it.

Grey Cloak and Dyphestive giggled.

The gnoll hit them both on the head with the rod and asked, "What do you find so amusing?"

"Stitches," Grey Cloak said. "A name for someone with one eye. Certainly you see the humor in it. It's so obvious." He looked over his shoulder. "No offence, Stitches."

Dyphestive fought to keep a snort in but couldn't.

"You'll have to forgive my fellow slave. He hasn't laughed in a long time, and now it's all coming out."

Stitches stormed forward. "They mock me! Let me kill them, Jumar the Gnoll!"

Grey Cloak erupted in laughter. "Knoll? You're named after a hill of dirt. I can't take it."

"Not k-n-o-l-l but g-n-o-l-l." Jumar snarled. "I, too, will not be mocked. What I think is the pair of you are nothing but thieves come to rob us. Well, we shall show you how we handle thieves. We cut off their hands and gouge their eyes out. Then we will see who laughs last."

Dyphestive and Grey Cloak got their laughter under control. The tide had shifted. Their predicament was no longer a joking matter.

But Dyphestive couldn't help himself. "You know, brother, if they cut our hands off, we're going to need stitches."

Grey Cloak burst out laughing.

"Enough!" Jumar said. "String them up!"

32

———

Back inside the pit, Zora fastened a collar around Streak's ankle and approached Anya. The Sky Rider sat against a dirt wall, clawing her fingers through her hair.

"What are you doing, Zora?"

"I'm putting the collar back on you so I can send you home." Zora snapped the collar around Anya's neck. "It's too dangerous here for you and Streak. Tell everyone back in the tower that we're fine." She turned the collar until she saw the emerald gemstone, which, when pressed, would activate the transport. She started to press the stone.

Anya blocked Zora's arm and said, "No you don't."

"This is for the best, Anya. They're going to kill you and Streak." Zora tried again to reach the stone.

Once again, Anya blocked her arm. "No," she said firmly. "The mission isn't over. I'm not going anywhere."

"You have to listen to me." Zora tried again, but Anya clamped both her wrists. "Ow! You don't have to break my arms."

The light in Anya's stormy eyes had returned. With her back braced against the wall, she stood. "Where is my sword belt?"

"I don't know. I imagine they seized it." Zora tried to pull free of Anya's iron grip. "Will you release me before you break something?"

"Stay away from my collar." Anya let go then turned the collar around her neck, hiding the gemstone trigger. "Where are we?"

"The Raiders' camp. You're prisoners, and we came to save you."

"We?"

"Grey Cloak and Dyphestive are outside, but they're prisoners too. We need to do something while we have time. But I don't have any idea how to wake Streak up. It might be best to send him back."

Anya took a knee by Streak's head and peeled back one of his eyelids. Only the yellow of his eye showed. "What did they do to him?"

"They drugged both of you with some sort of water." Zora picked her lip. "I don't know. But we need to make a move while the guards are distracted." She took a subtle step toward the collar on Streak's paw.

"Don't you dare."

"What do you think you're going to do? Lift him out of here?"

"I can wake him."

Zora crossed her arms. "And how in this world are you going to do that?"

Anya wiggled her fingers in the air. Wisps of lightning danced on her fingertips. Her wild eyes lit up like a burning sky. "You should stand back."

Backing against the wall, Zora said quietly, "She's crazy."

What has gotten into me?

Grey Cloak fought to control his laughter, but it didn't come easily. Perhaps the pressure he'd experienced over the years had finally caught up with him and he'd snapped.

The Raiders dragged him and his brother across the ground. To where, he didn't know. A cloudy sky loomed above, and drops of cold rain came down.

He laughed, stopped, then began laughing again. Numb to his grave situation, he was stretched out over the ground. His wrists and ankles were shackled with chains that pulled his arms and legs, stretching them to their full length.

He gave a nervous laugh and looked at his brother, who

was bound in the same situation. They made a pair of X's, underneath the torchlight in a moonless sky.

"I think this has gone on long enough," Dyphestive said.

"Are you referring to our current predicament or the whole thing?"

"I was referring to the moment at hand, but since you expanded it, well, I think you're right."

Grey Cloak strained to raise his head. He sought Jumar, who stood nearby while their chains were being tethered to horses. "I thought you were going to cut off our hands and poke out our eyes. What's this all about?"

Jumar spun the Rod of Weapons then tapped it on his shoulder. "As the king of the poachers, I'm at liberty to change my mind. Besides, life in the camp has been very dull of late. My Raiders need suitable entertainment. And it serves as a warning to any who would oppose me. So you will be quartered—pulled apart limb by limb. It sends a very..." He rubbed his hairy, furry chin. "Strong message."

"Well, anything you need to keep morale up," Grey Cloak quipped as the direness of his situation crept into his bones. He'd been buying time for Zora so that Streak and Anya could be relocated to safety, but he'd had no sign of that happening. "No sign is a good sign."

Jumar leaned forward. "What was that?"

"Nothing. I tend to talk to myself when I'm about to die."

With a grunt, Jumar flagged down his men with the rod. "Gather everyone around. We'll start with the quiet one. I want to hear him scream." He poked Grey Cloak's gut with the rod. "I'll save you for last. You make me laugh."

The soldiers moved the horses into position, and Dyphestive's arms and legs were spread out.

People gathered around. Children climbed on parents' shoulders. Horses snorted and nickered. Hooves clawed at the dirt.

"Brother, I was wondering—at what point are we going to make our escape?" Dyphestive asked.

Jumar dropped his arm and shouted, "Pull!"

The horses moved in four directions. Dyphestive's body rose from the ground, and he screamed.

"AAARGH!" Dyphestive belted. He wasn't in pain. He was angry, and he let it be known. "Auuugh!"

The horses leaned forward, struggling to take another step. Dyphestive pulled back, the muscles in his arms and thighs bulging. The metal cuffs tore into his wrists and ankles. Steel bent and groaned.

"What's happening?" Jumar shouted. "Pull that man apart! I want to see his bones!"

But Dyphestive's bones weren't those of a normal man. His were as hard as iron. It would take more than horses to rend them.

He set his jaw and growled. Veins rose like tree roots in his biceps.

One of the horses stepped back.

Unable to hide his astonishment, Jumar grabbed a lash

from one of his men and whipped the horse on its hind end. The beast reared.

Dyphestive gathered all of his strength and yanked.

With a loud whinny, the horse fell backward, and at the same time, a set of the links in the chain snapped. The beast toppled onto two soldiers.

The crowd screamed and scattered.

Grey Cloak summoned his wizard fire. His hands melted though the chains on his wrists. "Ah-ha, I'm free."

In that same instant, Dyphestive broke free.

The panicked crowd set off after the horse, and the two beasts tethered to Grey Cloak's legs bolted. They dragged him through the camp, across the rough ground.

"This was not part of the plan," he said as he fought his way up to a sitting position. "Ow, my backside." He reached for his toes, grabbed the metal cuffs on his ankles, and sent a jolt into them. The metal burst apart.

He rolled to a stop inside a cloud of dust, coughing and spitting out dirt. "Somehow, I didn't see it all happening that way." He hopped up to his feet and raced back to Dyphestive. "Rod of Weapons, here I come."

Dyphestive stood in the middle of a crowd of men, swinging his broken chains like whips and keeping the Raiders at bay.

Grey Cloak blindsided Jumar, leaped over the gnoll's head, and snatched the Rod of Weapons from his strong grip. He landed by his brother, fired up the tip of the spear, and asked, "Care if I join you?"

"The more the merrier," Dyphestive replied. A long length of chain whooshed over his head. "So, which side of the army do you want to fight? The left or the right?"

Grey Cloak reached into the inner pockets of the Cloak of Legends and drew forth the Figurine of Heroes. He set it down at his feet and said, "Let me see what I can do to even the odds first."

"Do you think that will work here?"

He smirked. "I'll take my chances." He muttered the incantation, and the figurine began to smoke.

BISH

DIRKLEN AND MAGNOLIA were marched up the gallows stairs at spearpoint. Their hands were bound behind their backs with rope, and they were under heavy guard. Members of the City Watch kept their crossbows pointed at them.

Georgio had warned them, "Any sudden moves, and you'll hang with holes in your heads."

Two nooses hung on the gallows. They were quickly fitted around their necks.

"I suppose you think I'm to blame for this," Magnolia said. Her eyes were wet with tears, and she sniffed.

Dirklen shrugged, determined to remain defiant to the end. "If I had to blame someone I know, I suppose it would be you. But please, don't cry. We're better than that."

"Better than that?" she exclaimed. "Did you ever stop to

think that maybe, just maybe, we chose the wrong side? And quit blaming someone else for your actions."

He scanned the faces in the crowd gathered in the city square. They were busy listening to the list of crimes they were being charged with. The list was lengthy, and they hadn't been in Bish very long, but they'd killed many.

"Humph," he said. "When I actually hear it with my own ears, it does sound rather bad. I never really kept count of all the people we killed."

"And you and I couldn't even name one we've saved." She frowned. "We've been selfish and spoiled all our lives. This is the price, I suppose."

"What were we supposed to do? Father was a commander of the Riskers. We were raised to conquer and serve Black Frost. Neither you nor I saw any wrong in it. It's a little late to play your violin of regret."

"I knew better," she said softy, gazing down. "Grey Cloak and Dyphestive were raised the same. Somehow they knew."

Dirklen rolled his eyes. "Do you really have to bring them up during my last moments? Grey Cloak is the reason we're trapped here in the first place."

"I always liked him. He had the cutest smirk."

He stuck his tongue out. "Now my stomach is turning." But his distraught sister had softened his heart. He cleared his throat and said, "You've been a good sibling. I know you didn't enjoy everything we did as much as I did. But I'm grateful you've always been by my side."

"Thank you. It's a little late, but it means a lot, brother. And perhaps if I'd shared my thoughts sooner, we wouldn't be strung up by a rope."

"No, Black Frost would have killed us if we betrayed him. If not him, Father would have. But now that I think about it, I wonder what it would have been like to fight on the other side."

As they were about to drop a black hood over Magnolia's face, she uttered her last words. "I guess we'll never know. Goodbye, brother."

"Goodbye, sister," he replied as another hood was dropped over his head, and his world turned black.

"I get their armor," Georgio said.

He stood at the back of the crowd, accompanied by Brak, Lefty, and Melegal, on the balcony above a store's front porch. They had a full view of the gallows and were joined by several crossbowmen on either side.

Melegal cleaned his fingernails with the tip of a slender dagger. "If you want that armor, you'd better fetch those bodies before the Royals become aware. I've already spied several picking their way through the crowd."

"I thought you had it taken care of," Georgio said.

Melegal raised his narrow shoulders. "I can only control what I can control."

Georgio grunted.

"Don't worry. I'll handle it," Lefty stated. The halfling sat on the balcony rail, kicking his little legs back and forth like a child. "I have a wagon ready. We'll lose the Royals when we take the bodies to the furnace."

"After all we've been through, I'm going to get something out of it," Georgio said.

"We have their swords," Brak said. He had Dirklen's and Magnolia's sword belts bundled up under one arm. "The steel is as fine as any I've seen, but the handles are too small for me."

Georgio patted the pommel of his sword. "I have a sword."

"Well, what do you want that armor for? You heal, unlike the rest of us," Melegal said. "Besides, you're too fat to fit into one of those suits."

"And you're too scrawny, even for the woman's," Georgio scoffed. "Besides, it's not for me. It's for my men. They need better equipment."

Melegal flipped his dagger over his hand, tucked it into a belly sheath, and said, "They need better leadership, if you ask me."

"Ha ha."

Melegal had been picking on Georgio since he was a little boy. Even though he'd grown thick skin over the years, the thief always had a prickly way of getting under it. "I hate to see a woman hang."

"A pretty one, at that," Brak added.

"What must be done, must be done."

From under his hood, Dirklen called in an agonized voice, "Mercy! Mercy!"

Georgio said over the murmurings of the crowd, "This is Bone. There's no such thing as mercy." Georgio nodded at the executioner standing behind the lever that operated the floor drop.

The executioner's hairy arms bulged as he yanked the lever back. The floor dropped beneath Dirklen's and Magnolia's feet.

The audience gasped. Two empty nooses dangled in the wind. Dirklen and Magnolia were gone.

Georgio took off his cap and scratched his head. "What in the Bish just happened?"

NALZAMBOR

INKY-BLACK SMOKE SPEWED out of the Figurine of Heroes and thickened.

The wide-eyed Raiders started to back away.

Strange fumes drifted through the camp while covering Grey Cloak and Dyphestive in darkness.

"Do you see anything?" Dyphestive asked. "I don't."

"Give it a moment," Grey Cloak answered. "I think I see someone."

The thick blanket of smoke began to lift as the evening breeze took it away.

A pair of newcomers stood facing the Raiders, wearing plate-mail suits of dark steel. Wavy blond hair flowed down to their metal shoulders. They carried no weapons.

"I can't believe my eyes." Grey Cloak shared glances with Dyphestive, who rubbed his jaw. "It's not them, is it?"

"I think it is. Dirklen? Magnolia?"

Magnolia turned and gasped when she laid eyes on Grey Cloak and Dyphestive. She tilted her head and rubbed her enchanting eyes.

Dirklen dropped to a knee and kissed the ground. "We're alive!" He grabbed handfuls of crabgrass and ripped them out of the ground then tossed them upward. "We're saved!" His eyes met Jumar's. "Do I have you to thank for this, ugly, dog-faced man?"

Magnolia grabbed a handful of Dirklen's hair. She lifted him up to his feet and turned him around. "No, I think you can thank them."

Dirklen stiffened, balling his fists up by his sides, and his once-jovial face reverted to his natural scowl. "You! I swore I'd kill you if I ever had the chance!"

"Before you try that, you might want to take a closer look around," Grey Cloak said. "You see those hundreds of people? They're here to kill all of us."

Dirklen twisted around and said to Jumar, "I'm not with them." He pointed at Grey Cloak and Dyphestive. "You can have them. I'd be glad to help you!"

"What about turning over a new leaf?" Magnolia asked. "After all, he saved us."

"I don't care."

Jumar eyed them all. "More tricks! Clever tongues filled with deception. You fooled me once. You won't fool the king of the poachers again. Summon the gray-scalers. The dragon riders of the sky. Kill them!" he ordered. "Kill them all!"

Dirklen and Magnolia backed away from the army and joined Grey Cloak and Dyphestive.

"What have you gotten me into this time, Grey Cloak?" Dirklen demanded. "Every time I see you, I'm standing on death's door."

"Maybe if you'd quit whining and start fighting, we can all get out of this."

"Fight your own battles, elf!" Dirklen reached for the Rod of Weapons. "Give me that!"

Grey Cloak shielded the rod with his body. "Get your own weapon."

Magnolia joined Dyphestive. "Will the two of you stop bickering?"

Battle horns sounded, and dragon riders dropped out of the sky.

"We need to fight together if any of us are going to survive this!"

"Agreed," Dyphestive said.

"We can beat them if we join forces." Grey Cloak extended his hand. "Truce!"

Dirklen pointed at Grey Cloak. "Only until the battle is won." He shook Grey Cloak's hand firmly. "Then we shall talk again." He faced Jumar and cracked his knuckles. "It's been a bad day." Lightning flickered in his eyes, and cords of energy snaked around his arms. "Who shall I take it out on first?"

Jumar drew his sword, raised it over his head, and said, "Attack!"

Grey Cloak stood with his back to Dyphestive. Magnolia was to his right and Dirklen to his left, creating a box defense formation. "Stand your ground, everyone, and let them have it!" He pointed the Rod of Weapons at the enemy, summoned his wizard fire, and let out pulses of bright balls of energy.

The fireballs spit out in rapid succession, hitting the three closest Raiders and knocking them over one after the other. He didn't stop there.

Their attackers' ferocity turned to timidity. They scrambled to find shields and hid behind one another.

Grey Cloak pelted them with balls of fire, sending them screaming and running with their hair and clothing alight.

At the same time, thoughts raced through his mind. *Dirklen and Magnolia won't remain permanently. But they only need to be here long enough for us to win or the enemy to give in.*

While firing, he glanced over his shoulder.

Both Dirklen and Magnolia had stripped their attackers of their weapons.

Magnolia wielded a halberd and filled the head with wizard fire. Using broad, sweeping strokes, she cut through the Raiders' ranks, and they fell in heaps.

Dirklen had taken a pair of long swords and moved them as one. The steel blades burned with a life of their own, and he cut through men like they were made of butter.

Behind Grey Cloak, Dyphestive hefted an orc in full armor over his head and hurled the man into a pack of attackers, bowling them all over.

Many had fallen, but many more came.

In the same way Grey Cloak used the Rod of Weapons, Dirklen and Magnolia turned their fire loose from their blades.

"Show them our might, sister!" Dirklen shouted. "Make them rue the day they encountered the likes of us!"

Jumar hung back with his mouth hanging open. He howled like a wolf and screamed, "They're making a mockery of us! Where are the dragons? Summon the dragons!"

Battle horns sounded. The thunder of dragons' wings beating erupted in the air. They swooped in and landed, crushing their own men underneath their talons.

Four dragons squared off against Grey Cloak, Dyphestive, Dirklen, and Magnolia. Behind them, more dragons landed with riders. Each dragon, called a gray-scaler, was little bigger than a horse and had smooth gray skin like a snake. They all let out frightful roars.

Dirklen laughed. "You call that a roar? What sort of winged-lizards are they anyway?" He pointed his swords at the closet one, which was approaching him. "They look like ugly chickens to me." He unleashed his fire, striking the dragon in the hard scales of its chest and knocking the rider from the saddle. The hot metal of his sword started to bend. "What sort of cheap steel is this?"

The dragons didn't wait to answer his question.

Jumar barked, "What are you waiting for? Charge!"

The dragons crept closer, maws opened wide. Bolts of lightning came out, striking Grey Cloak, Dyphestive, Dirklen, and Magnolia in their chests.

Dirklen and Magnolia were knocked backward and into one another so hard that their metal armor crashed like cymbals.

The Cloak of Legends reflected the hit on Grey Cloak, but Dyphestive was knocked head over heels. He let out a growl, charged the nearest dragon, and socked it in the jaw. The creature wobbled and collapsed to the dirt.

Dirklen and Magnolia scrambled back to their feet, and the dragons started to crowd them.

Grey Cloak backed toward them. "Everyone together!"

"We need to spread out," Dirklen said. "We're as dead as a goose if we stand in one spot!"

"Much to my surprise, you make a good point, but I have another plan," Grey Cloak said as he fed more wizard fire into the rod. "Dyphestive, stay close!"

Dyphestive walked backward toward them.

Grey Cloak had never tried it before, but he was going to create a protective dome like Tatiana had done for them on occasion. "I might need you to feed your energy into the rod if we're to hold them off. Grab on!"

As they reached for the rod, the glowing orb that had stunned them before dropped from the sky.

Grey Cloak had a split second to react. Using his rod like a club, he swung at the globe.

The glimmering ball exploded with a concussive force of energy that blew through the camp.

He fell to his hands and knees, his ears ringing. His limbs were like noodles, and the ground felt spongy. *That wasn't a wise move.*

Dirklen glared at him. "What have you done?" He shook Magnolia, but she was knocked out, slumped on the ground.

Only Dyphestive was still standing. He'd picked up Magnolia's halberd and swung at everything that moved toward them.

The enemies fell, but it wouldn't last. There were too many men and too many dragons, and the ones that still had their senses after the stun bomb were closing in.

With the Rod of Weapons in hand, Grey Cloak summoned his energy once more, but the blue flames spit and sputtered from the tip. "Zooks, I hate it when that happens."

36

JUMAR MARCHED TOWARD GREY CLOAK, baring his canine teeth. "I'm not even going to make you suffer! I'll feed you to the dragons instead. Your last breath has come!"

What had been a steady rain shifted to a downpour, and the ground turned to mud. Lightning streaked across the sky.

Grey Cloak looked up. He still had plenty of fight in him, with or without the wizard fire, but he spotted a better option. He smirked at Jumar. "Perhaps it would be best that you surrender before it's too late."

"Don't mock me!"

A thunderclap sounded. *Boom!*

Streak dropped out of the clouds with Anya riding on his back. A stream of lightning danced on her sword. He dove straight toward the gray-scalers with yellow fire in his eyes. He blindsided them and turned loose his fiery breath. Swooping around in a tight circle, he created a ring of fire, burning the dragons and their riders.

The gray-scalers screeched, beating their flaming wings. They took to the sky, but the fire ate through the membranes of their wings, and they collapsed.

"No!" Jumar shouted. He shook his sabre at the sky. "No! Go away! You're my prisoner!"

Anya locked eyes with the gnoll, and Grey Cloak stepped away from the dog-faced man.

A thick cord of lightning came down from the clouds, struck Jumar, and blew his body into pieces. The hard rain washed what was left of the bone, armor, and patches of smoking hair away. The king of the poachers was dead.

His army fled, and before long, the entire camp had been abandoned by man, orc, beast, and dragon.

Dirklen woke his sister up as Streak and Anya landed.

Zora appeared beside Grey Cloak. "What are they doing here?" She nodded at Dirklen and Magnolia.

"That's a good question. I used the Figurine of Heroes and much to my dismay, they came. I don't know what happened, but they should have vanished by now."

Dyphestive tossed both halves of a broken halberd aside. "Perhaps it's this world."

"It's a glitch," Streak stated.

Grey Cloak gave him a funny look. "What are you talking about?"

"The term was coined in the other world I visited. A glitch happens when something doesn't work the way it's supposed to."

"Makes sense," Grey Cloak replied.

Anya approached Dirklen and Magnolia. "I say we kill these wretched glitches."

"Back off, Anya. We made a truce." Grey Cloak turned to Dirklen. "Assuming you still want to keep it."

Dirklen kept his wary gaze on Anya. "I do."

"We do," Magnolia said.

"You can't be serious. You can't trust these snakes. They're Riskers!"

"I don't think they're going to do anything stupid, unless they want to be trapped on this world. Besides, there are more of us than there are of them. I believe they'll behave," Grey Cloak said. "Now, let's find our gear and move on before the Raiders have a change of heart. The farther we get from this place, the better." He helped Magnolia to her feet. "Streak, scout ahead."

"Aye, aye, boss," the dragon said.

Grey Cloak added, "Anya, you might want to go with him."

Her nostrils flared as she sheathed her sword. She glared at Dirklen and Magnolia. "Make one false move, and I'll turn your skulls into birds' nests." She turned and walked away.

Dirklen gave Anya an approving nod and said, "So, that was the last of the Sky Riders. Huh. I like her."

The company resumed their journey to Dark Mountain. They walked all night and the next day, distancing themselves from both the rain and the Raiders' camp. Finally, they stopped late in the evening of the next day and settled down by a fire.

Dirklen and Magnolia had tended to trail behind the group, talking quietly to each other.

With a four-point buck on his shoulders, Dirklen made his way into camp. He lowered it to the ground and said, "Dinner for everyone. Who wants to skin it?"

"Why don't you skin it?" Anya asked.

"Because I don't have a knife. For your safety, Grey Cloak thought it might be best that we didn't have any weapons. Not that we need any. Besides, the weapons in that camp were little more than scrap." He eyed her sword belt. "Nothing like the dragon steel you carry. Would you like to skin the buck?"

"No, I'd rather skin you," Anya said.

Magnolia chuckled.

Dyphestive approached. "I'll skin the beast. Besides, I'm hungry." He fished a dagger out of his belt and dragged the carcass away.

"I'll help," Magnolia said as she pushed her way back to her feet. "If you don't mind."

"Of course not."

An awkward silence followed. Anya was out of sight, sitting on the other side of Streak, who lay near the tree line with his eyes closed. That left Grey Cloak and Zora alone with Dirklen.

Dirklen absentmindedly touched the ugly scar that ran from his eye down his cheek. He was a fit warrior, a full-grown man with a short blond beard and a strong chin. With or without armor, he was a man who was as formidable as they came. He caught Grey Cloak staring.

"Admiring my cheek, are you? It's courtesy of Black Frost for our failure at Monarch City. You remember that, don't you? The day my father died."

"We weren't asking for a fight," Grey Cloak answered. "We were only trying to stay alive."

"Oh, I know. I remember that day every minute of my life. The scar, you see, always burns." Dirklen broke a small stick and tossed it into the fire. "Such is the kiss of Black Frost."

Grey Cloak was tempted to apologize, but he didn't. Instead he said, "You have another chance, you and your sister, to get it right. We're here to find a way to destroy Black Frost before he destroys all of us, including you, first."

Staring into the fire, Dirklen snorted. "Destroy Black

Frost. A dragon as big as a mountain." He thumbed his scar. "I can't believe I'm going to say this, but I'll help."

Grey Cloak and Zora shared quick looks of surprise.

"Forgive my boldness, but why the change of heart?" Grey Cloak asked.

Dirklen glanced at his sister. "We've had some earnest chats of late, and we agree. The way of Black Frost is death. We want life. Freedom." He lay down by the fire and looked into the sky. "It's something we've never had."

"That's what we all want. That's why we're here, in another world."

Dirklen nodded. "So, tell me—what are we looking for here?"

"Something called the Apparatus of Ruune."

Closing his eyes, Dirklen said, "Sounds wonderful."

37

THE NETHER REALM

ZANNA HAD STARTED to regret her decision to learn more about Utlas the speaker of the realm. He hadn't stopped talking since the conversation began days ago, as he led her on an unending tour of the city.

On a positive note, he'd allowed her mystic bonds to give her a little more mobility so that she could keep up with his giant strides. She still shuffled her feet on the grimy paved roads, but it was an act. She didn't want him to think she had more mobility than she did.

Utlas stopped in front of a dried-up circular fountain with a strange humanoid statue on the top. The figure towered over him. It had a round, almost insect-like head with oversize probing eyes and a well-defined body with sculpted muscles and strange wings, like a moth's, on its back.

"Did you make that?" she asked.

Utlas tilted his long, gaunt face over to one side and said, "Oh no. I have no idea who made it nor what it is, but I have always liked it. What do you think it is?"

Zanna scratched an ear and said, "I don't know. Some sort of moth man?"

He massaged his chin. "Interesting." He strolled on.

The listless, gargoyle-like people wandering the streets parted from his path.

Zanna lumbered after him with her wrists locked in front of her and her shoulders slouched, appearing to be exhausted. Her belly moaned. It had been a long time since she'd eaten. Taking quick, shuffled steps to catch up, she said, "I don't mean to sound ungrateful, but my feet are tired, and I'm hungry. Is it possible that we can stop so I can refresh myself?"

"Yes," he said in his deep voice, which was more like a moan. "I forget your frailty. Your skin will adapt to this world in time. The soles of your feet will be as hard as old leather."

She grimaced.

Utlas snapped his fingers, and a small, stout humanoid hurried to the giant. He had a full beard that hid most of his face. Small white insects crawled in it.

Zanna's face soured.

"Utay, my guest wishes to eat. Bring proper food suitable for her. And a bottle of wine."

Utay bowed, and bugs flew out of his beard. "As you wish, Utlas." He hurried away.

Zanna wanted to object, but she held her tongue. The sight of Utay's beard had eradicated her appetite.

Utlas led her through the vast city and climbed the stairs of the palace. He sat down by one of the great burning urns at the top and patted a spot beside him. "Sit, Zanna. We'll have what they call a picnic. Only the two of us."

She sat and said, "You're most kind. And I'm thankful for the tour. It's revealed the talents in the Realm."

"It's garbage. Refuse. A land without hope. I hurt for my people."

"Then it's time we found a way out. We need to speak about Black Frost. No matter how strong he is, he has a weakness."

He crossed his massive hands behind his head and said, "I'm all ears."

Utay appeared at the bottom of the steps and ambled his way to the top. He set down a tray of tarnished silver platters along with a dusted bottle of wine then bowed and hurried away, vanishing into the palace.

Zanna looked at the discolored platter and the bottle of wine. The dusty green bottle was sealed with a cork. As far as she could tell, it was a dark-red wine. But the dome covering the platter captured the most of her attention. She couldn't help but stare.

I don't think I want to know what might crawl out from under there. Perhaps a coiled serpent waits to strike. Maybe bugs or poisonous spiders will crawl out and devour my hide or lay eggs under my skin.

"I thought you said you were hungry." Utlas grabbed the handle on the dome. "Please, help yourself."

Zanna's lips curled back as he lifted up the lid, but only crackers, cheese, and fruit awaited underneath.

The tightness in her chest eased. "Thank you," she said. "I have to ask—how do you grow grapes? The land doesn't appear fertile, as far as I can see."

"The Nether Realm is vast. In places, the soil is rich, and streams run through the rock and dirt." The wine bottle looked tiny when he picked it up. He pulled out the cork and poured until her goblet was half full. "Sadly, most of our delicacies were not portioned for the likes of me. But I'm not much of an eater or drinker. Please, enjoy yourself. I'm very interested to hear what you have to say."

She ate. The food satisfied her appetite, but the grapes were more sour than sweet. Gazing up at the fiery sky, she washed a mouthful of food down with wine and asked, "Can't you dig underneath the Flaming Fence?"

"We tried. It goes too far down."

"What about the streams? They have to pass through somewhere."

Instead of answering her question, he said, "Tell me more about Black Frost."

"He fears the dragon charms. That's why he has spent decades gathering them and keeping them dispersed. It's why he hasn't had the Helm of the Dragons destroyed and buried. I believe you had the right idea to turn it against him, but you need a better plan." She sloshed her wine around in the goblet and gulped a large mouthful. "You need to find a way out of here. There has to be a way. He'll never suspect it, and once you have the advantage, you strike."

Utlas gave her a bored look, but a glint of interest lurked in his solemn gaze. "You believe the answer is in my clutches?"

"I believe as long as you have the helm, Black Frost won't ever let you go."

38

A LITTLE BIT of good could be found in the worst places. The red wine was sweet on Zanna's tongue. She dabbed her lips with a napkin. Half the bottle was gone, her cheeks were warm, and she felt a little tipsy.

Utlas sat on the top landing with his arms hanging over his knees. "I see you're enjoying the cuisine."

"That wine is fine," she said and hiccupped. "Do you have any more?"

"We have plenty. Shall I call for Utay?"

She shook her head. "I'd prefer it if you didn't. His appearance might spoil my appetite."

"You'll get used to it."

"I know I can get used to this." She set down her goblet and picked up the bottle of wine by the neck. Then she stood, drank like a sailor, and wiped her mouth on her sleeve. "Where to now?"

Utlas managed a feeble smile. "Since we're talking about the Helm of the Dragons, I think it's a good time to visit the chambers."

"The chambers?"

"A storehouse of rare artifacts. I think you'll find them interesting. And we can speak about the secrets of the helm. I assume you understand its ways," he said.

Zanna took another sip. "I know why it was created. And you've seen it at work. All the dragon charms working in harmony to control many or control one the size of many?"

He stood. "Come. We will talk about it."

She fought to keep up as they entered the palace. Utlas moved at a brisk pace, and her mystic bonds limited her. Four soldiers of the condemned followed them inside. They'd been escorting them from a distance the entire time.

The palace halls were massive, built for giant men like Utlas. She could barely see from one end to the other.

Utlas turned down a corridor that sloped downward into subterranean levels and stopped at a vault sealed by iron doors. A quartet of gargoyle-like sentries were posted outside the door. He waved his arm.

One of the sentries used a ring of keys to open the three

locks that secured the door, then he and the other three sentries pulled the doors open.

Utlas and Zanna walked inside.

The deep vault contained weapons racks and suits of the finest armor—leather, scale, ring mail and plate suits fit for the races of all shapes and sizes. Chests full of treasure —coins, rings, necklaces, precious gems, and pearls—filled the floor. Bull whips and an assortment of hats hung from pegs on the walls. Contraptions with wings hung from the ceiling. Trinkets and baubles were scattered loosely on the tabletops and had spilled to the floor. The vault was worth a hundred times a monarch's ransom, if not more.

"Where did all this come from?"

"These are our spoils from the world above." Utlas picked up a brass wrist cuff studded with gems. "My wife gave me this," he said solemnly. "A symbol of our bond. She's long gone."

"Should I ask what happened?"

"No."

She wandered through aisles of treasures. The vault reminded her of Batram's Bartery and Arcania. She picked up a strand of rubies and diamonds. "This is breathtaking."

"You can have it, if you wish."

"Why would you give me such a thing?"

Utlas raised his eyebrows. "It's something you might as well enjoy while you can." He set down the brass cuff and moved toward the rear of the vault with his arms crossed behind his back.

The Helm of the Dragon sat inside a large nook in the back wall. All the colorful gemstones were intact. It was the most brilliant and captivating object in the room.

Zanna took a swig from the bottle. The open-faced helm was a perfect work of metal craftsmanship by wizards—like her husband, Jerrik Paydark. She took a breath.

"What are you thinking, Zanna?" Utlas asked.

She crinkled her nose and said, "I wonder how well it really works. I mean, how hard is it to control? They say each dragon charm has a mind of its own. Does that make sense?"

"Perfect sense." Utlas picked it up. "Why don't you try it?'

"Me?" She shook her head. "I couldn't."

"You understand the mind of a dragon better than a Sky Rider."

She stared at the helm for the longest time. It beckoned to her.

He's testing me. I know it.

She turned away. "I can't."

He patted her on the head and put the helm back. "Well done. You will make a fine slave."

39

THE WIZARD WATCH

BLACK FROST'S dragon took Gossamer and Zanna Paydark —disguised as Datris—to the nearest Wizard Watch in Ugrad, south of Dark Mountain. It was the same tower they'd departed from to quicken their journey to Dark Mountain.

They circled the tower, which stood in a bleak landscape of fields of leafless trees and black bark. Then the dragon stretched its wings out and made a soft landing, roaring.

They dismounted, Gossamer first, with Zanna following.

Without so much as a glance back at them, the grand dragon took off at a sprint, beat its wings, and vaulted into the sky. In moments, the dragon's tongue could kiss the clouds, where it disappeared.

Gossamer's heart raced. It had pounded the entire time they were in the air. "I can't believe it." He gazed over the tower. "We made it."

She slapped him on the back. "You did well." Knocking on the tower walls, she said, "I hope you can get us inside this place."

Gossamer passed his hand across the stone archway entrance, and the wall vanished. He stepped aside. "After you."

The exquisite fountain in the center of the entrance chamber had dried up. They walked past and took the sloping corridors that led to the top.

Talon had entered the Wizard Watch in the south, below Arrowwood. But all the towers were connected and of a similar fashion. They were designed to be portals from one territory to another so that the Wizard Watch could keep an eye on the affairs of the world.

They made it to the higher levels, where the Chamber of Murals' entrance waited. The door was closed.

Gossamer took a breath. "Please be in there."

"Who are you talking about?"

"Tatiana and Dalsay. I don't think I can handle many more surprises."

"It'll be fine." She squeezed his shoulder. "Open it."

"I'll have to knock."

As he uttered the last word, the slab of stone opened,

and Tatiana came rushing out. She gave him a strong embrace and almost lifted him. "You made it!"

He nodded. "This is Zanna."

Tatiana took them both by the wrist and dragged them inside. "Hurry. The moment you entered the tower, we were alerted. Dalsay and I have prepared the portal so that you can send her back in time."

Inside the Time Mural chamber, Nath sat on the edge of one of the pewter thrones with his hair hanging over his eyes. Dalsay stood behind the Pedestal of Power, his face a mask of concentration. The Time Mural was a swirl of colors that began to solidify to a vision of the snowy north in Ice Vale.

"I need to change you back into you, Zanna," Gossamer said.

"Please, the sooner the better. I miss my body."

He summoned his wizardry, took her hands, and chanted the incantation. Warm energy flowed back and forth between them. Datris's face turned into Zanna's beautiful countenance right before his eyes.

Zanna smoothed her hands over her body. "Ah, that's so much better. I have curves again." She kissed Gossamer on the cheek. "Well done." She walked in front of the Time Mural and asked, "So, this is it?"

Gossamer nodded.

"I wish Jerrik were here to see it."

"Are you ready?" Gossamer asked.

"Yes, you've told me everything I need to know. I'll find Grey Cloak and Dyphestive in the dungeons of Ice Vale. Don't worry. I know my way around a jail cell."

Nath swiped the hair away from his face. "Good luck, Zanna."

She gave him an odd look and nodded. "Thank you, hermit."

Tatiana had joined Dalsay behind the pedestal. "The portal is ready. Go now."

Without a word, Zanna stepped inside, and she was gone.

Nath leaned back in his chair and said, "I can't wait to see what comes out of that portal next."

Gossamer's back muscles eased. He'd done it. He closed the time loop and sent Zanna back to the place she needed to be. They were on track. "Where are the others?" he asked.

Tatiana replied, "Grey Cloak, Dyphestive, Anya, Zora, and Streak are in Nath's home world, searching for the Apparatus of Ruune. We await their return."

"Return? Don't you have to summon them?"

"We can, but we've made modifications to their collars that will allow them to return on their own," Tatiana said as she watched the snowy image in the Time Mural cool into a wall of stone. The surrounding gemstones no longer glinted.

"That's brilliant. But how long can we afford to wait?"

"It won't be forever. We plan to summon them back one at a time, if need be."

"What about Zanna? Is she still trapped in the Nether Realm?"

"There has been no communication with her whatsoever. We're lying low, but the other members of Talon are outside, camping in the fields."

"We need to save her," Gossamer stated.

Tatiana shook her head. "It will be too risky with two Zannas in the same time. We have to defeat Black Frost first. Then we can go after her. I'm sorry. I see no other way."

"And I agree," Dalsay added.

Gossamer understood. "I think I'll head outside and get some fresh air." He eyed Nath. "Care to join me?"

"Certainly. It's time I stretched my scaly legs," Nath said in a raspy voice. "They're getting as stiff as brittle wood."

40

THE NETHER REALM

Zanna sagged against the wall and clutched her stomach, groaning.

"What is wrong?" Utlas asked.

"My stomach." She slid to where the Helm of the Dragons rested. "It aches. Was the food you gave me poison?"

Utlas stiffened. "I did no such thing. Though it is an acquired taste. Your body will need to adapt to it."

She fell to all fours and started to regurgitate something. "Water," she pleaded. "I need water."

"You will have it." Utlas snapped his fingers. "Sentries, fetch fresh water."

Zanna spit out a small metal object, which bounced on the stone floor. She picked it up.

He bent over and asked, "What is that? Did you eat it?"

She studied the metal band, which had the shape of a ring, and slipped it on her finger. "It's a gift from a dear friend of mine."

"And you ate it?"

"My stomach was the safest place I could put it." She pushed her way up the wall, easing one hand toward the helm, and said, "I feel a little better now. I only need to steady myself, but water would be nice."

"Tell me about this ring," Utlas demanded.

"My husband gave it to me. Much like the metal wrist cuff your wife gave you. It is precious to me."

"Really? And you store it in your stomach for safekeeping? That's odd. Why not wear it?"

"I've always feared someone might take it. I hope you don't mind if I wear it now." She touched the rim of the helm and kept her back toward Utlas, looking over her shoulder.

Utlas's head tilted from side to side. "I see no harm in it if it brings you comfort."

She nodded. "Thank you."

A sentry entered the vault carrying a metal decanter. He set it on the floor at Utlas's feet, bowed, and hurried away.

Utlas picked up the decanter. Water sloshed over the rim when he spotted Zanna, who was cradling the Helm of the Dragons in her hands. "What are you doing with that? Put it back."

"I will when I'm finished with it."

"What do you mean?"

"I'm going to use it to destroy Black Frost."

"Oh, is that so? And how do you propose to do that when you can't leave?"

"Because the ring on my finger isn't from my husband but a teleportation ring from my friend Gossamer." She held it up. "Thanks for bringing me to the Helm of Dragons. See you later, Utlas. I'm going home, while you burn in yours."

"No!" He dropped the decanter, and water splashed over the floor.

"Oh, and let's keep this secret between us. I don't think you want Black Frost to learn about your favor." She winked. "Bye, now." In a moment, she blinked out of sight, with the sound of Utlas's outrage resounding in her ears. Her world spun in a myriad of colors.

Nath grabbed Gossamer by the arm as they made their way through the chamber's exit. "Hold on. Do you feel that?"

Gossamer's skin prickled, and he turned around.

Tatiana and Dalsay were the only other people in the chamber, but he sensed another presence.

"What is it?" Tatiana asked.

Zanna Paydark appeared, holding the Helm of the Dragons.

Gossamer's heart leaped. "Zanna! Can it be, or do my eyes deceive me?" He rushed to her.

"It's me in the flesh." She wiggled her fingers, showing off the teleportation ring. "Our plan worked. You should have seen Utlas's face. If he was miserable before, I can only imagine how much more miserable he'll be now that he's been duped. Giant fool. I got him good."

"Interesting. I thought you departed moments ago," Nath said.

"What are you saying?" Zanna looked at Gossamer. "Did you send me back to Ice Vale recently?"

"Only moments ago. Today must be my day. Everything has worked out, and the loop is closed."

Zanna tossed her head back and laughed. "I can't believe it." Letting out a long breath, she eyed the others then held up the Helm of the Dragons. "Look, I've brought a present." She gave Gossamer a stiff embrace, handed him the helmet, then put her hands on her hips. "So, where're my son and Dyphestive?"

Nath pointed his scaly finger at the Time Mural.

She raised an eyebrow. "Care to fill me in?"

Tatiana walked out from behind the pedestal and joined her on the main floor. "We couldn't be certain that we would retrieve the helm. Nath offered an idea. There is a weapon in his world, the Apparatus of Ruune. We believe it could destroy Black Frost."

"We have the helm now. Bring them back," Zanna said. "There's no sense in wasting any more time. We need them now."

"Two weapons are better than one," Tatiana stated. "We're giving them more time. They can return when they're ready, or we can summon them back when need he. We have a plan. We'll stay with it."

Zanna faced the mural. "If you say so. But now I can see why my son was never so enamored with you. I think I'll head outside. I've missed the fresh air, and it's become rather stuffy in here."

"I'll join you," Gossamer set down the helm on one of the thrones. "The others will be elated to see you and hear the good news."

41

NALZAMBOR

"WHAT ARE WE LOOKING AT? It's a river of fire," Dirklen said as he stood on a ledge, looking into a chasm. "My chin hairs crinkle."

Grey Cloak heard him, but his attention was elsewhere. He held the map that Nath had made and was staring at the Mountain of Doom. He compared the picture on the parchment with what was in front of him. It was the largest mountain he'd ever seen. Its central peak pierced the misty clouds.

"This is the place we're supposed to find the stones," Dyphestive said as he peered at the map from behind Grey Cloak.

"It's a starting point." Grey Cloak rolled up the map. "A big starting point." He turned his attention to the river of fire that surrounded the mountain like a moat. "It's no wonder only dragons lived in there. There's no way into the mountain unless we fly. Streak, it's time for you to take us over."

Streak sat on the ledge several yards away, staring into the streams of molten lava. He shrugged his wings and said, "Fine by me, but you'd better hang on, because that's one hot bath you don't want to take." He tilted his head from side to side in quick, birdlike moves. "Where do you want me to take everyone?"

Grey Cloak pointed. "That lower ledge. Nath said there's an entrance at the bottom. We'll find it there."

"And I'll do some flying around and see what I can see." Streak lowered his body. "Load up. I think I can handle three or four at a time."

Anya and Zora joined Dyphestive in the first group to fly over, then Grey Cloak flew over with Dirklen and Magnolia. The twins dismounted on the other side, but he remained in the saddle.

"I'm going to circle and see if I can find the entrance. This way will be quicker."

"What do you want us to do?" Zora asked.

"Scout the area. You never know what you might find. For all we know, the entrance could be right under your feet." He tugged the reins, and Streak took flight.

"Do you think that's a good idea? Leaving them alone together?" Streak asked.

"Dyphestive will keep the peace if Dirklen starts up."

"If he can't?"

"Well, if he can't, then I guess they'll kill one another." He leaned right, and they soared along the mountain. "Get a little lower. Nath said it was closer to the base."

Streak nodded.

The Mountain of Doom was barren. No trees or even a shrub grew in the rocky soil, and no moss grew on the shadier side, either, making it easier to spot any sort of entrance.

A natural groove twisting through the ravines caught Grey Cloak's eye. It snaked through the rock.

"Land there," he said.

"Aye, aye, boss." Streak turned his wings and made a soft landing.

The channel wasn't wide enough for the dragon to fit, but Grey Cloak dropped down into it. "I'll see where this goes and be right back."

Streak shuffled his clawed feet along the rim and followed him.

The channel bored through the rocks and came to a dead end at the mouth of a small cave. Faint markings in the rock outlined a door. The symbols were not familiar.

"This is it," Grey Cloak said. He felt for an edge to the door inside the markings but found nothing. "Well, I found it, but Nath never said anything about needing a key. Streak!"

"Yes, brother?" the dragon answered, his voice echoing down the channel.

"I think I found it! Bring the others. I'll try to find a way to open it in the meantime." He ran his fingers over the runes that outlined the doorway and blew dust out of some of the patterns. He stood on tiptoe, reached up to the top, and touched more patterns. Nothing seemed familiar. Then he remembered. "Ah, Dyphestive has Nath's signet ring. Perhaps that will do it."

Grey Cloak searched the engravings, looking for the face of a dragon that would match the ring.

"No, I don't see anything that vaguely resembles it." He put his hands on the wall, dipped his head, and sighed.

So much had happened, and it was the first time in a long time he'd had a moment to himself. He needed time to think.

"Gather yourself, Grey Cloak. You can't doubt yourself now. You must see this through."

He thought about those who had come and gone: Adanadel and Browning, Grunt the Minotaur, and Jakoby and Leena. Then he remembered the Sky Riders who'd trained him: Justus, Hammerjaw, Slomander, Yuri Gnome-knower, Aric the elf and his sisters, Stayzie and Mayzie, and Gorva's father, Hogrim. So many had fought and died for the right cause, yet he still lived.

Have I forgotten any? Shame on me if I did.

Countless more dragons, men, and women had died for the cause of freedom.

I won't let them die in vain. They died so that I could live and finish this.

He sat down, closed his eyes, and waited.

And I will finish this once and for all.

Streak brought everyone to the secret channel, where they all gathered in front of the door.

"What a wonderful dead end you've found," Dirklen said. "Marvelous."

Magnolia nudged him. "Be supportive."

"I'm here, aren't I?"

"You're welcome to search elsewhere if you wish, Dirklen," Grey Cloak said as he towed Dyphestive to the door. "Take all the time you like."

Zora chuckled.

Streak managed to snake his head into the gap. "Say, I think I can fit through there."

"Stay put," Grey Cloak said. "We might need you for a hasty exit, if we can make it in." He held out his hand and cleared his throat. "Dyphestive. The signet ring."

"The what? Oh." Dyphestive fished the necklace from his tunic.

Everyone gawked at the ring.

"What is that? A dragon face?" Magnolia asked. "Pretty. Why don't you wear it?"

"My fingers are too big," Dyphestive answered. He removed the ring from the chain and handed it to Grey Cloak. "You try it."

Slipping the ring on, Grey Cloak walked up to the outline of runes. He traced the ring along the runes without touching them. "Nothing is happening."

"What did you expect to happen?" Dirklen asked.

"I thought a door would open."

"Yet here we stand."

Zora gave Dirklen a disappointed look and said, "You aren't very mature for a grown man, are you?"

Magnolia laughed. "I don't think it's a matter of maturity. He's getting old and cranky, like an old man."

"I'm barely thirty seasons," Dirklen whined.

"Closer to forty."

"So are you," he retorted.

"True, but I handle it more gracefully."

Anya pushed through the group and asked, "Do either of you know how to man up or act like a true woman warrior?" She pulled her sky blade and pointed it at the door. "Stand back. I don't have time to listen to the prattling of babes."

Grey Cloak jumped back. "Anya, no!"

But it was too late.

Loud thunder cracked in the sky, and a bolt of fire shot out of her sword and struck the face of the stone wall then died, leaving a black mark on the wall.

Everyone uncovered their ears and eyes. Aside from the scorch marks, the wall showed no noticeable damage.

"Well, that was helpful," Dirklen stated. "Perhaps you'd have better fortune using your hard skull like a battering ram."

Anya sheathed her sword and said, "Better yet, perhaps I'll use yours."

Dirklen slid back as she walked away from the door. His eyes followed her the whole way. "I have mixed feelings about that woman."

"Yes, we all do," Zora said.

"Why's that?"

"Because she's crazy."

Grey Cloak tossed the ring to Dyphestive. "I don't know. You try it."

He caught the ring and said, "Like I said, it won't fit."

"Did you try it?" Zora asked.

He held up his sausage-sized fingers. "What do you think?"

"Try your pinky, donkey skull," she said.

"Hm." Dyphestive put the ring on his pinky. "Snug fit but a fit. So, what should I try to—*uck!*" His body stiffened like a board, and his eyes rolled up into his head until only the whites showed.

"Festive!" Grey Cloak cried in alarm.

His brother became a catatonic automaton, marching to the door. Skin crawling, Grey Cloak stepped out of Dyphestive's path.

"Festive?"

Dyphestive stared at the wall blankly.

Grey Cloak waved a hand in front of his brother's face and snapped his fingers. "He's out of it."

"If you ask me, he's always been out of it," Dirklen said.

"Don't say that," Magnolia scolded him.

"He's weird."

"I like it. I find his demeanor sweet and endearing. It would be awful if he turned out like you. No offense."

Dirklen's mouth hung open.

Suddenly, Dyphestive started to speak in a strange language. The words rolled off his tongue, captivating everyone like a beautiful song and wrapping them in a warm embrace.

Zora squeezed Grey Cloak's hand. "How is he doing that?" she whispered.

"It must be the ring."

"The words are music." She leaned on his shoulder. "The likes I've never heard before."

Grey Cloak eased against her. It felt like the two of them were melting into one. Whatever his brother was saying, he liked it. They all did. He glanced over his shoulder and caught Anya wiping tears from her eyes.

Suddenly, the symbols around the edge of the door glowed with golden light, and the mountain began to open.

"Look," Grey Cloak said in a hushed voice.

As Dyphestive spoke, the stone wall faded until a dark tunnel appeared.

Still holding Zora's hand, Grey Cloak towed her inside. "Come on, everyone."

Dyphestive remained in a deep trance, but the majestic words came to an end. Sweat glistened on his face. His eyes dropped down, and he swayed.

Grey Cloak and Zora wrapped their arms around Dyphestive and guided him into the tunnel.

"Are you well?" Grey Cloak asked.

"What happened?"

"The ring took over."

Dyphestive broke away from them. "I'm fine. As a matter of fact, I feel really good." He raised his hand and looked at the ring. The emerald and ruby eyes twinkled like tiny fireflies. "Huh."

"What is it?" Grey Cloak asked.

Dyphestive pointed into the corridor. "I think it wants me to go that way."

"Nath said the ring would help us find the Thunderstones." Grey Cloak moved aside. "Lead the way, brother."

"Hey!" Streak yelled from outside the entrance. He'd

managed to squeeze his body into the channel and brace his face against the frame of the opening. "What about me? I want to come."

"You're too big. Wait for us."

Streak hung his head. "Aw, I wish I could shrink again. Life seems more fun when you're smaller."

Grey Cloak went back and put his hand on Streak's nose. "If I could still fit you in my hood, I would."

Streak frowned. "Would've, could've, should've, whatever." He laid his head on the ground and closed his eyes. "Wake me when it's over."

43

USING the Rod of Weapons as a source of light, Grey Cloak led the company into the depths of the mountain. Dyphestive walked by his side, swinging his arms and gazing at the lofty ceiling.

"These tunnels are humongous. Who needs tunnels this big?" Dyphestive asked.

"Dragons," Dirklen commented. "They aren't so much bigger than the corridors that led into the dragon kennels in Dark Mountain."

Dyphestive replied, "The dragons squeezed through those tunnels like lizards. These are big enough for grand dragons to walk through, with two or three abreast."

Magnolia chimed in, "Perhaps giants lived here."

"This is Dragon Home. I don't think dragons and giants got along in this world either," Dyphestive answered as he slowed down and joined her. He offered her a friendly smile. "But it's a good suggestion."

Magnolia hooked her arm in his. "Thank you, Festive. How nice of you to say."

Dirklen leaned toward Zora and said, "I think I'm going to vomit. She has awful taste in men."

"A shame she didn't get a choice in brothers." Zora hurried to catch Grey Cloak.

Anya brought up the rear, but Zora caught a smile on her face. Once Anya caught up to Grey Cloak she asked, "Mind if I join you? The enormity of this place makes me uncomfortable. And what if we run into dragons? Don't they live here?"

"We can only hope they're sleeping." He nudged her. "But this place is fascinating. It reminds me of Hidemark, where the Sky Riders trained. But bigger."

"What do you expect? It's an entire mountain," Anya commented. "A mountain as big as Gunder Island."

Chunks of rock had fallen and blocked off part of the passages.

Grey Cloak scuffed the debris-covered floor with his boot. "Look at this." The floor was made with unique paving stones that were bigger than men's feet. "It's a road inside the mountain."

They traveled onward until the tunnel split three ways.

Anya made her way to the front and asked, "Now what do we do? Split up?"

"I don't think that's a good idea," Grey Cloak said.

"Dyphestive," Magnolia said, "look at your ring. It's glowing."

"It's doing more than that. It's nudging me." Dyphestive broke away from Magnolia and stood at the intersection. "Nath said the ring would help us. I think we need to follow it." He stepped toward the tunnel on the left, and the ring cooled. "No, not that way." He moved to the tunnel in the middle, which sloped upward, and the dragon eyes brightened. Then he stood in front of the tunnel on the right, which made a level passage into the mountain. The eyes in the signet ring dimmed. He pointed into the middle tunnel. "This is the way."

"Are you sure?" Grey Cloak asked.

Dyphestive raised his shoulders. "The ring is the only surety I have. I trust it."

"Lead the way, then."

The long walk began. They turned down corridors that seemed to flow with the natural curvature of the mountain rather than having a purposeful pattern. Passing many open chambers, they never stopped to look in. Dyphestive led them onward at a brisk and steady pace.

Zora stayed close to Grey Cloak the entire time. Her shoulder brushed against his often, and they helped each other over the broken chunks of ceiling that blocked the passages. Her hands were warm when they touched. He welcomed it.

They passed through a chamber large enough for a town. Little square apartment-like buildings were built into the stonework. Firepits were scattered over the ground, but there were no signs of coals or the scent of burning wood lingering.

"Some people must have lived here with the dragons," Anya said as she bent over and picked up a staff of wood. She used it to stir some of the old coals in a nearby pit. "I wonder where they went."

"Maybe the dragons ate them," Zora suggested.

"What dragons?" Magnolia asked. "We haven't seen so much as a sign."

Zora rubbed her shoulders. "It feels like a mausoleum. Nothing has moved through here in a hundred years but us."

"A hundred years or much longer," Grey Cloak said as he looked about. "But we aren't here for that. We're here for the Apparatus of Ruune. Let's go."

Dyphestive took the lead again.

After over an hour of walking, they came upon a tremendous pair of metal doors sealed shut. The doors stood over twenty feet high and were decorated with ornate images of dragons made of brass. A luster still shone through the dingy spots. Grey Cloak rubbed some of the grime away.

The ring on Dyphestive's finger burned brightly. "This is it. I can feel it in my bones."

All of a sudden, the light in the ruby and emerald eyes of the ring went out.

"What happened?" Grey Cloak asked.

Dyphestive shook his hand. "I don't know. It went cold."

"Perhaps it served its purpose," Zora suggested.

Grey Cloak nodded. "I think you're right. After all, we're here."

"What are we waiting for?" Dirklen asked as he marched to the doors. "Let's go in."

Dyphestive clamped a hand on Dirklen's shoulders. "We need to be cautious. Nath warned us of a guardian that protects the stones."

"We'll have a listen," Grey Cloak said. He put his ear to the door, and Zora joined him. His eyes were fastened on hers, and her eyebrows twitched. "Do you hear what I hear?"

"Yes," Zora replied, surprised. "Someone is singing."

44

A STRONG VOICE resounded on the metal doors, and Grey Cloak heard every word almost as clearly as if he were standing on the other side. Whoever was singing did so with pep as they belted out one tune after the other.

He and Zora couldn't help but smile.

Fascinated, Grey Cloak listened more and beckoned for the others to join him.

Over hill, over dale, ugly giants always smell,
As the warriors of Morgdon march on.
You can tell by their stench, there is trouble on the trail,
As the warriors of Morgdon march on.

· · ·

For it's hi-ho-ay,

> *The time has come to slay.*
>
> *Lift up your axes and pints of ale.*
>
> *Anywhere we go,*
>
> *The giants always know*
>
> *The warriors of Morgdon march on*
>
> *Keep a-stompin'.*
>
> *The warriors of Morgdon march on.*

Dyphestive wore a grin as wide as a river. Even Dirklen's smug face cracked a smile.

The songs kept coming, and the chuckles did too.

The ugliest orc I ever saw

> *Was sipping pond water through a straw.*
>
> *The ugliest orc I ever saw,*
>
> *Was sipping pond water through a straw.*

I crept up on him with my axe,

> *His nostrils flared. He pulled a blade.*
>
> *I crept up on him with my axe,*
>
> *His nostrils flared, and he pulled a blade.*

· · ·

The battle started. The fight went on.
  I stuffed his face in the murky pond.
  The battle started. The fight went on.
  I stuffed his face in the murky pond.

The scrap was over. I had won,
  I took his head and buried it.
  The scrap was over. I had won,
  I took his head and buried it.

The ugliest orc I ever saw,
  No longer sips through a straw.
  The ugliest orc I ever saw,
  Is buried in a murky pond.

With her ear pressed to the door, Anya said, "I like this dwarf. I want to meet him." She grabbed one of the massive brass handles and started to pull.

"No, wait," Grey Cloak said. "He's still singing. Let him finish."

"He might not ever finish."

"A little discretion. We don't want to spook the little man. He might help us."

"He might be a guardian and want to kill us," Zora said.

"I think we can handle a singing dwarf," Dirklen commented.

I am Brenwar. I like to drink ale.

And when I drink ale, I do it better than all my kind.

I am Brenwar, and I like to slaughter titans.

And when I slay them, I do it better than all my kind.

"He sounds formidable," Dyphestive said.

"All dwarves sound formidable," Dirklen replied. "I've never met one that didn't think they could slay anything."

"Anya, are you a dwarf?" Zora quipped.

Anya gave her a deadpan stare and said, "Do I look like a dwarf?"

"No, but if I close my eyes, you sound like one."

Everyone fought to keep their chuckles in check, but Dyphestive erupted in laughter.

"Shh!" Grey Cloak warned him as he fought to keep his own laughter in check. "We don't want to alert him."

Dyphestive took a breath and avoided Anya's stare.

Putting his ear to the door, Grey Cloak raised his hand. "I don't hear anything."

"Go in. Knock if you want. He must have heard us," Dirklen said. "What are we waiting for?" He grabbed the handle and started to pull.

"Agreed." Anya tugged the other handle.

Zora tapped Grey Cloak on the shoulder. "Proceed with caution." She lifted the Scarf of Shadows over her nose and vanished.

"Good idea," he said. "No sense in alerting him to all our presences. At least some of us are keeping our heads."

Dirklen and Anya puffed and grunted. The doors wouldn't budge.

"They must be locked on the other side," Magnolia said.

"Let me try," Dyphestive said.

As Dirklen and Anya stepped aside, he seized the handles in his mighty grip and squeezed. He dug his boots into the floor and leaned into the pull. He huffed, and his face turned as red as a beet. The veins in his muscular arms bulged.

"Use your legs," Grey Cloak said.

"I am!" Dyphestive grunted.

"He's not strong enough," Dirklen said.

The doors groaned, and the handles started to bend. They broke off, and Dyphestive stumbled backward. He fought to stay on his feet then slid to a stop with his knees bent.

"Well done. You broke the door. Now how will we get in?" Dirklen asked.

"There must be a locking bar on the other side," Grey Cloak said as he eyed the crack in the doors. "I think I can see it. Dyphestive bent it."

Suddenly, the doors moved, and everyone stepped back. They were bathed in golden light, and everyone shielded their eyes.

Grey Cloak peered inside. "Zooks."

They slowly moved forward and stood at the threshold of the greatest treasure hoard he'd ever seen. As far as the eye could see, the floor of the massive chamber was covered in piles of shining coins, twinkling gems, precious jewelry, and assortments of gorgeous items.

"This can't be real," Magnolia said as she wandered farther in. "It must be a trap."

Dirklen picked up a golden coin the size of a small saucer and flipped it. "Oh, it's real." He bit it. "I can taste it. As sweet as honey."

Grey Cloak's attention passed over the treasure and stopped on a great stone chair toward the back of the chamber. The chair had no arms and was big enough for a giant to sit upon. Instead, a dwarf stood on the throne with a war hammer resting on his brawny shoulders.

The dwarf spoke in a voice like rolling thunder. "You're going to fix my door, then you are all going to die." He jumped down from the chair and marched toward them.

"On second thought, you're going to die first, then I'll fix the door. I like fixing things. It's the only way to get it right." He brought the hammer over his head and started to bring it down. "Prepare to die, gold burglars. Face the might of Brenwar Boulderguild!"

45

THE FLAT OF Brenwar's war hammer hit the ground with a *krackow*! The ground jumped, and piles of gold heaved into the air.

Everyone lost their footing and lay on the floor, covering their ears.

A shockwave blew through Grey Cloak's body, seeming to turn his guts inside out. He struggled to regain his feet and slipped over the coins as a pile of treasure tumbled over him.

Dirklen made it to his feet first and faced off against the oncoming dwarf, whose beard was full of braids.

"Nobody robs a dwarf! Come and get some, pretty boy!" Brenwar bellowed.

Dirklen scoffed. "You shouldn't underestimate me, you runt of a man!" Fire flared on his fingers, and he picked up a spear stuck nose down in the treasure. Lightning strands snaked around the tip and the shaft, and he hurled it at Brenwar.

Brenwar batted the spear with his hammer, creating an explosion of fiery light. He stood his ground and said, "Ha!" Then he rushed forward.

Grey Cloak wormed his way out of the pile. "Back off, Dirklen. We didn't come to start a fight. We can talk."

"You shouldn't have come at all!" the dwarf roared. He barreled into Dirklen and knocked him to the ground.

They wrestled over the war hammer.

Dirklen tried to wrench it free. "Don't hurt yourself, dwarf. I'm stronger than you."

"Is that so?" With one hand gripping the handle, Brenwar jerked Dirklen eye to eye with him. He shook the handle like a rug, making Dirklen's teeth clatter. Then he lunged forward and cracked Dirklen in the jaw with his forehead.

Dirklen sagged to the ground.

Brenwar kicked him in the gut. "Don't forget to pick up your teeth!"

Dyphestive plowed through a pile of coins and tackled Brenwar into a mound of jewelry.

"Ah, a little giant." The dwarf attacked Dyphestive like a wolverine, hammering him with hard punches to the gut.

Wide-eyed, Dyphestive doubled over and groaned, "Oof!"

Brenwar's fists were covered in steel gauntlets. He hit so hard that ribs cracked. "How's that for a rib tickler, Giant Boy?"

Lightning sprayed from Magnolia's fingertips. Tendrils of energy pierced Brenwar's metal breastplate. His eyes turned white, and his beard began smoking.

"How does that tickle?" Magnolia asked with fire burning in her eyes.

"Dwarves don't tickle!" He stretched his arm out. "And don't mess with my beard!"

On its own, his war hammer flew end over end then struck Magnolia from behind. She went down in a heap.

Brenwar caught the war hammer, and with his body smoking all over, he said, "Now my mouth tastes funny. Nothing some dwarven ale won't wash down. Who's next?"

Anya moved toward Brenwar at full speed. "You talk a lot for a dwarf. More like a gossiping woman than a fighting man!" She hacked at him with her sky blade.

"What?" He parried with his war hammer.

Metal rang on metal, and sparks spit in the air. *Clang!*

"Ho ho, and you fight like a bearded gnome! Fool woman, no one bests Brenwar Boulderguild." He popped her gut with the handle of his war hammer and launched a headbutt into her chin. *Clack!*

Anya fell over on her side.

"Good night, warrior woman!" Brenwar bellowed. "I bet

you've never been kissed by a dwarven lullaby before. Ho ho! Enjoy yer nap!"

Zora, the invisible spectator, had hung back long enough. Brenwar was mowing down her friends like a sickle in a wheat field.

What is this dwarf made of? Perhaps something subtle will do. She twisted the Ring of Mist on her finger. *Here goes nothing.*

Brenwar moseyed across the chamber, whistling and grunting a cheerful tune.

Zora moved into his path. The tiny metal flower petals of the Ring of Mist opened and sprayed him in the face.

"Ack!" Brenwar smacked his lips. "Who doused me with perfume?"

"I did," Zora said as she reappeared.

"Ah, a part elf." He glowered at her. "A mighty stupid thing to do. Dwarves don't stink. But elves do!" He cocked back his war hammer and let loose a powerful swing.

Grey Cloak jerked Zora out of harm's way before the war hammer clobbered her skull.

"That was bold." Grey Cloak pushed Zora behind him. "Now let me give it a try."

The Rod of Weapons flared into a shiny blade.

"Great anvils, another elf," Brenwar grumbled. "And I

thought all of them were dead. You know what they say. Where there's one, there're dozens more cowering in the weeds." He hefted his weapon onto his shoulder, spit into his hands, rubbed them together, and said, "This won't take long."

"Brenwar Boulderguild, we didn't come to fight or steal!"

"The time for talk is over!" Brenwar attacked.

Grey Cloak jumped backward and blocked at the same time. "You never gave us a time to talk. You attacked. Let me explain."

"No problem, robber. You can explain all you want when I put your skull in my collection!"

Grey Cloak stood his ground, gritted his teeth, and fought back.

46

GREY CLOAK TRIED to use his speed to his advantage, poking and jabbing at the dwarf's face and legs.

The skilled fighter used his war hammer with deadly precision, blocking every one of Grey Cloak's attacks with quick strokes.

Brenwar Boulderguild proved to be a tireless warrior, thrusting himself into the action as fearlessly as a charging bull. To make it worse, he sang in a dwarven tongue as he fought, thoroughly immersed and enjoying himself.

"You must listen to me, dwarf," Grey Cloak said as he jumped backward onto a heap of gold. "We mean no harm!" He leaped over the swing of the war hammer. "Please, listen!"

The surefooted dwarf stormed up the slippery pile of

coins like a mountain goat. "Stand still, elven rodent. Mortuun wants to say hello!"

"Who is Mortuun?"

"Why, that's the name of my war hammer. Thanks for asking!" Brenwar brought down an overhand chop and smote the pile as Grey Cloak hopped away. "What are you? A cricket?"

"Zooks on this!" Grey Cloak dropped the Rod of Weapons down, mustered all of his wizard fire, and shot out a string of energy balls. "Aaauuugh!"

The energy blasted into Brenwar like a barrage of snowballs. He smacked away the first one but caught the next five hits in the face and chest. He came off his feet and landed in a treasure pile on the other side of the aisle.

Flattened against a pile of coins, which were cascading over his body, Brenwar lay still. The war hammer slipped from his grasp and into the aisle.

Grey Cloak leaped down into the aisle and approached with the tip of the Rod of Weapons ready.

Zora joined him, and the others—all walking wounded —ambled over.

"Is he dead?" Zora asked.

Dirklen rolled his shoulders and said, "I volunteer you to take a closer look."

"I'd rather not. He nearly took my head off once."

"We didn't come here to kill him," Grey Cloak said as he

drew closer to Brenwar. "He's not the enemy. I hope he's not dead."

Zora shot him a look. "He almost killed all of us. He'll do it again if he's alive. Isn't that what guardians do?"

"I don't know. What do you think, Dyphestive?"

Dyphestive rubbed his jaw. "He makes me think of Rhonna."

"Me too."

Grey Cloak spotted the finer hairs in Brenwar's moustache. They didn't stir, and his chest was still. Dousing the fire of his staff, Grey Cloak said, "I don't think he's breathing. I didn't want to kill him. If he wakes, we'll ask questions."

"If he wakes," Magnolia said as she arched her back. "A large part of me hopes he stays asleep."

Anya stood over Brenwar. "He was a formidable warrior. A match for all of us. He deserves a proper burial."

"I wonder if Nath knew him," Grey Cloak said.

Solemnly, Dyphestive replied, "He never mentioned anything about a dwarf to me. He only said there would be a guardian protecting the Thunderstones or the Apparatus of Ruune." He tilted his head as he stared at Brenwar. "Though I did expect an opponent much bigger. But he fought like a giant. I've never been hit so hard. My skull is still ringing. And my bones are iron." He rolled his jaw. "I think his skull is as well."

"Everyone gather around," Anya said. "I'll say a few words, and we'll find a proper tomb to bury him in."

"Say a few words?" Dirklen's face soured. "He tried to kill us."

"Respect your enemies," Anya replied. "Though in your case, I might not bother."

"I don't think he was an enemy," Magnolia said with a sad expression. "He only did what he was meant to do. And look around. Someone has to guard all this treasure."

"Enough. Get on with it, Anya," Grey Cloak said.

Brenwar's blazing eyes opened. "Boo!"

Everyone jumped back a full step.

The dwarf sat up and broke out in laughter that resounded throughout the chamber. He slapped his knee and said, "Only a dwarf buries a dwarf." He eyed them all as he combed his stubby fingers through the braids of his beard. "I haven't had this much fun in centuries. Ho ho! So, tell me, who are you children?" He scooted down the pile of treasure and reached for his war hammer.

Grey Cloak flamed up the Rod of Weapons.

Brenwar eyed him. "If I wanted to kill you, I'd have killed you already, but we can all have another go at it, if you like." He picked up the war hammer. "But Mortuun and I won't show mercy this time."

Grey Cloak doused his flame. "So now you want to talk?"

"Not really. Talking's for elves." Brenwar set down his

weapon handle up and rested his hands on the butt of the shaft. "You mentioned Nath. How do you know him?"

"How do *you* know him?" Grey Cloak asked.

"I'll ask the questions."

Dyphestive took off the ring and gave it to Brenwar. "He said this would help us find the Thunderstones. We need them to save this world and ours."

Brenwar held the ring up to his face and inspected it like a jeweler. "Where is Nath?"

"On our world," Dyphestive answered.

Brenwar groaned. "He's alive?"

"Yes, but he's dying."

"Dying? What's happening? Is his hair falling out?"

"It's gray, mostly. His body is aging. He looks like a hermit. A big hermit but a hermit," Dyphestive said.

"A hermit, you say. Never thought I'd see the day. Of course, I've been guarding the king's throne room for more decades than I can count. It is my charge. The sole purpose I live for."

"Who is the king?" Grey Cloak asked.

Brenwar eyed the throne. "Why, Nath is, of course."

"Isn't that throne a little big?" Zora asked. "The old hermit couldn't even climb up it."

"Watch your tongue, elfie, or the next time I swing, I won't hold back and miss."

Zora swallowed and moved away from the brooding

dwarf. "He really doesn't like elves, does he?" she whispered to Gray Cloak.

Grey Cloak nodded at Dyphestive. He had a feeling Brenwar would rather deal with his brother than him.

"Brenwar, can you help us find the Thunderstones?" Dyphestive asked.

"Help you? I'd do anything for Nath. He's my friend. He's the dragon king. I've served the dragons all my life." He lifted the war hammer and pointed it around the room. "They're in here somewhere."

Dirklen eyed the trove. "You don't know where they are? It'll be like finding a needle in a haystack."

"That's the idea behind hiding them, dimwit."

"Are we really supposed to believe you don't know where they are?" Dirklen fired back.

"My, aren't you as snotty as an elf," Brenwar said. "No, I don't know where they are. What do you think I do? March around all day, taking inventory?" He moved away and started whistling a new tune.

The company glanced at one another.

Finally, Grey Cloak said, "The stones aren't going to come to us. We'll split up into teams and start looking." He eyed the staggering amount of ground to be covered. "Zora, come with me."

47

GREY CLOAK and Zora stood behind the throne, wading through the treasure, as Brenwar peered at them from the seat.

"Brenwar, have you seen the stones before?"

Brenwar called down, "Of course."

"And what do they look like?"

"Marble eggs with brilliant colors." He made a shape in the air with both hands. "Yea big, like my fist. Smoothed-over eggs with a rune carved in them. Pretty."

"Thank you. At least they're bigger than a needle." Grey Cloak dug through piles of coins like a dog digging a hole. "Did you find one yet?" he quipped to Zora.

"Funny." She wiped her forehead on her forearm. Standing knee deep in wealth, she put on a necklace made of sapphires and diamonds as big as teardrops. "How does it look?"

"Dazzling."

"What? This old thing?" She tossed it aside. "It's already out of style." She picked up another one. "How about this one or this one?" Her hands were filled with sparkling jewels. "I don't know whether to be sick or flabbergasted."

He chucked a lantern made of solid gold aside and asked, "What do you mean?"

"There's so much treasure. I mean, what do you do when you have so much? What would you spend it on if you had everything?"

"Good question. I think sometimes when you have nothing, you want everything, and when you have everything, you want nothing. Does that make sense?"

"I suppose. If we had all this treasure, we'd always be worried someone might steal it. Then we'd have to pay a grumpy dwarf to guard it."

"I heard that," Brenwar said.

"Do you ever leave?" Grey Cloak asked.

"No. If I leave, I die. This is my purpose. This is why I'm still alive after all these centuries."

"And no one comes to visit?" Zora asked.

"Not in the normal sense. Strangers come. They don't go. Keep digging around. You'll find their bones."

Grey Cloak picked up a skull made of solid crystal. It

was twice as large as his head and oblong. "Is this from a real person?"

"Aye. A real dead person."

Dirklen rummaged through a heap of silver coins and crystalline baubles. He and Magnolia were separated from the others.

He whispered to her, "We need those collars. Look around for a weapon we can use so that we can get them."

"Are you out of your skull? You gave your word. We help them, they help us."

"Don't be a fool. They won't help us."

"Of course they will. They'd have killed us if they wouldn't."

Dirklen found a small, well-crafted dagger with a pearl grip and tucked it into his sleeve. "As soon as we return, they will imprison us or subject us to some sort of authority. And I don't care what weapon they built. It won't be enough to destroy Black Frost. He's invincible."

"Do you want to be his stooge forever?" Her eyes shot daggers at him. "This is our chance to make things right. Start a new life."

He found another dagger and handed it to her. "Are you with me or not, sister?"

She took the weapon and hid it inside the plate of her

armor. "I'd do anything for you, brother. You're all I have. But you should trust me on this. Let your grudge go. It will destroy you."

He glowered at Talon working far across the way. "Not if I destroy them first."

"Ah-ha!" Anya shouted. She held up a Thunderstone. "I found one!" She turned it over and gave a funny look. "At least I think I did."

Peering at her from the throne, Brenwar shouted, "Aye. That is the Thunderstone of Power. That's the one I'd pick, if I had a choice."

Dyphestive, who stood nearby, said, "Well done, Anya."

"Yes," she replied, "and that only took how many hours?"

"Ha, it's been so many. Who can keep count? At least we've found one. That gives me hope." Dyphestive came across a painting half buried in a treasure pile and dug it out. It was a portrait of a stunning woman with flowing platinum hair in front of a starry sky. He held the large picture out. "I wonder who this is."

Anya moved beside him. "You aren't seriously asking me, are you?"

"Huh, no."

"She's a striking beauty. I'll give her that." Anya

stretched her fingers out. "Her porcelain skin looks so real that I think I could touch it. Not a blemish, wrinkle, or mark on her. Doesn't look like she's done a day of hard work in her life. I don't think she was a real person. Probably a figment of some man's imagination."

Dyphestive nodded. "Perhaps. But she looks real to me. I feel like she's staring right through me."

Anya took the painting and set it aside. "Let's get back to work." She bumped him. "Leave the staring to me."

He grinned and dug into the treasure.

48

Grey Cloak dropped a gold-plated shovel, placed his hands on his back, and arched backward. "Ahh!"

He and Zora had made their way toward the back of the chamber and were digging along the back wall, which was filled with a great painting of dragons on the earth and in the sky. Grey Cloak had never seen the likes of them. Some dragons had scales like pure gold, and others had scales as smooth as polished silver. They came in all sizes, from that of a bird to as big as three grand dragons.

The painting had chipped off in places, and cracks and creases spidered throughout. Grey Cloak stared for the longest time.

"What's the matter?" Zora asked as she drew close to him. "Have you given up?"

"Huh? Oh, no. It's this mural. I swear it's moving,"

"I try not to look. I feel like they're staring at me." Her eyes were fixed on a tremendous red dragon with scales flecked with gold. It dominated the scene, flying over lush grasslands filled with armies from all of the races. She pointed at a towering, redheaded warrior standing on a cliff face and looking up at the great dragon with admiration. "I wonder who that is."

Grey Cloak shrugged. "I suppose the dwarf knows. Care to ask?"

"No, but he caught my eye. He's handsome."

The image of the warrior was as big as they were, but it had deteriorated and faded.

"That caught your attention?"

"There's something about the way he's standing. Something good and noble about him."

Grey Cloak straightened his back, stuck out his chest, and raised his chin. "How does proud and noble look on me?"

"Good but not quite as good as him."

"You're harsh."

She grinned. "I have to be me."

"Indeed. Come on. Let's go see how the others are doing." He led the way toward the throne, where Brenwar sat with his short legs hanging over the edge. His head followed them as they moved.

So far, they had found three of the five Thunderstones, one from each group, but the hours had been long and turned into days.

"What are you doing? Taking a break?" Brenwar asked as they walked by the chair.

Grey Cloak replied, "If you don't mind. Isn't that what you're doing?"

"Dwarves don't rest."

"It looks like you're resting to me," Zora said.

Brenwar picked up his war hammer and stood. Glowering at her, he asked, "Does it look like I'm resting now?"

She grabbed Grey Cloak's arm and whispered, "If he weren't a dwarf, I'd swear he was Anya's father."

"I heard that," Brenwar said.

"Does she even have a father?" Grey Cloak quipped. "I always thought she was born in a den of wolverines."

"My father is dead, thank you," Anya said.

Zora gasped and clutched her chest.

Anya had crept up behind them. She tossed a Thunderstone to Zora. "I found another one. How many does that make?"

"Ettin's ears, that makes four!" Grey Cloak said. "Well done, Anya."

She turned and walked away.

"Do you think we hurt her feelings?" Zora asked.

"No!" Anya barked.

Brenwar's laughter rumbled from above.

Grey Cloak spun around and noticed more loose piles of treasure under the throne. "Let's take a look over there."

"I don't see why not," Zora answered. "There's probably been a Thunderstone under there all along."

Two stone tables near the throne had treasure heaped up around their bases.

Grey Cloak found a tremendous sword unlike any he'd seen before. It had a huge double-edged blade and a double handle wrapped in leather. The cross guards were fashioned with the faces of two dragons. One had emerald eyes, and the other had eyes like rubies.

"Dyphestive!" he yelled. "You have to see this!" He reached for the sword.

Brenwar dropped from the throne and landed on a pile. "Don't touch that."

"Is it yours?" Grey Cloak asked.

"No, it's Nath's."

"The hermit?" Zora asked.

"Aye, that's his sword, Fang. If you touch it, you will die."

Grey Cloak pulled his hand back.

Dyphestive arrived. His eyes grew the moment they landed on the sword. "Whoa!"

"I told you it was something," Grey Cloak said.

Dyphestive nodded. "I've never seen the likes of it. Wait a moment." He lowered the signet ring toward the blade. The small gems in the ring and the sword's cross guard started twinkling.

"Humph. Fang speaks. Interesting," Brenwar said. "He's been cold for the longest time. He misses his creator."

"He?" Zora asked.

"Aye." Brenwar clawed at his beard. "Fang has a mind all his own. But he can be fickle like a woman at times."

A bow lay on the other stone table. It had no string, and the ends of the shafts were curled inward. Zora asked, "Is this Nath's too? It looks broken."

"That's Akron. Not broken," Brenwar replied. Sadness fell upon his countenance, and a tear came to one of his eyes. He caught everyone staring. "What are you gawking at? Don't you have a Thunderstone to find?" With that, he marched away.

MAGNOLIA FOUND the last Thunderstone inside a wooden treasure box filled with pearls and sapphires. "Look," she said to her brother, who had his back to her.

He turned, and his eyes widened. He peeked over a heap of treasure, spotted the positions of the others, and hurried to her side. "Hide it."

"Why?"

"Because I said so. That's why. Here." He snatched it out of her hand.

The marble stone was green like an emerald with a glow that lit up the seams of marbling within. He eyed the runes engraved on the stone. "I wonder what sort of powers it can unleash. I can feel its energy inside my veins, as if my wizard fire is amplified."

"I felt the same thing with the other stone we found too.

What are you suggesting, brother?" she asked in a harsh whisper.

He looked over his shoulder and said, "Now is when we make our move. We catch them off guard, take them out, use the collars, and go home with the Thunderstones. We give them to Black Frost as a trophy. Surely he will reward us greatly."

"Brother, you are mad. Let your grudge go. I like these people."

"Black Frost will destroy them. You know that. He is as big as a city." He narrowed his eyes on her. "Are you with me or not?"

Magnolia sighed and nodded. "I always have been, and I always will be. What's the plan?"

He spied on Grey Cloak and Zora, who were gathered by the throne with Dyphestive. "The half elf, Zora. She keeps the Thunderstones inside her satchel. I'll use this stone to strengthen my powers. When we're close enough, I attack. You fetch the satchel and her collar. I'll take Grey Cloak's." He showed his dagger. "Once I kill him."

Brenwar stood before them all with a large rolled-up parchment. "You've recovered four of the five stones, and I imagine it's only a matter of time before you find the last. The yellow is the Stone of Power, blue is for thought, pink for command, orange for sight, and green for transport, which is still out there." Brenwar pushed Fang aside and started unrolling his parchment. "I don't dally with the magic, but my kind built this."

"I thought you said Fang would kill you if you touched him," Grey Cloak said.

"We're friends. As I was saying, you'll have to build the Apparatus of Ruune and feed the stones into these chambers." Brenwar ran his pudgy index finger over the draft of the apparatus. The contraption was larger than a horse and sat on four legs. It had a narrow but bulky body like a wagon and a long metal tube shooting out from one end.

Everyone tilted their heads and looked at it.

Brenwar continued, "Think of a ballista. Aim and fire. Nath should know what to do." He poked his finger at the intricate lettering all over the draft. "These are the details. Any questions?"

They shook their heads.

Brenwar rolled up the oversize scroll, bound it with a letter cord, and handed it to Dyphestive. "Don't lose it, little giant. Yer plans will be ogre dung if you do."

Dirklen and Magnolia moved closer to the throne.

Grey Cloak caught Dirklen's shifty gaze and spotted the last Thunderstone in his grip. "I see you found the final piece of the puzzle. We have everything we need and can leave now."

Magnolia eased over to Zora's side and clasped her

wrists in front of her. "You can return, but how will we return?"

"Simple. We will send someone back with two more collars," Grey Cloak said as he reached for Dirklen's stone. He opened his hand. "You can trust us. We've trusted you this far."

Dirklen stretched out his hand and pulled it back. "I have a suggestion. Why don't you take Magnolia back on the first trip, and one of you can remain with me."

Anya replied, "That's not going to happen, you little worm. You should count your blessings that you're still breathing. If it were up to me, you wouldn't be." She turned her burning stare on Magnolia. "Nor would you."

Dirklen stiffened then took a breath and said, "Fine. You win. After all, you have been more than fair. But can you blame me for looking out for my sibling's interest? Wouldn't any of you do the same?" He offered the stone to Grey Cloak. "Take it. I only want to go home."

"And I miss my peace and quiet," Brenwar said. "All of you chatter like a bushel of halflings."

Dirklen gave his sister a subtle look.

Grey Cloak's attention shifted toward her. A bead of sweat rolled down from her temple. Conflict filled her face.

The fire in the green Thunderstone flared.

"Dirklen, no!" Magnolia shouted. She pushed Zora away. "Everyone, watch out!"

"Traitors!" Dirklen's face turned into a mask of rage. "I

shall kill you! I shall make you pay!" His entire body glistened with an emerald-green sheen, and a pulse of energy burst from his body, knocking everyone to the ground.

All of them climbed back to their feet, and Grey Cloak made a quick head count. Everyone was there but Dirklen.

"Search for him," he said.

"He's gone," Brenwar replied.

"What do you mean, 'he's gone'?" Grey Cloak asked.

"He used the Stone of Transport. It swept him away."

"Swept him away to where?"

"Anywhere he wanted. Anywhere he's ever been." Brenwar climbed back to the top of the throne. "I think your friend was right. You should have killed him. Your mission will be far more difficult now."

Streak peeked into the throne room. "Hello? Did you forget about me? Whoa! Look at this hoard!" He strolled inside with a smile like a crocodile's, sweeping his two tails behind him. "Why the long faces? You've discovered the greatest treasure I've ever seen." He looked up at Brenwar. "Look, a gnome."

"Gnome?" Brenwar grumbled. "Get that lizard out of here!"

Streak reared. "Lizard? Who are you calling lizard, you bearded halfling!"

"That's it." Brenwar stood up with Mortuun. "I'm eating lizard for dinner tonight!"

"Enough! Both of you." Grey Cloak looked at the

disheveled Magnolia. The color had drained from her rosy cheeks, and she hung her head. "Where do you think your brother went?"

"I'm sorry. I tried to get him to see right." She gave Grey Cloak a pleading look. "But he would not be persuaded. After all you've done for us, his pride wouldn't allow him to let go of the grudge. If he went anywhere, he went back to Dark Mountain to warn Black Frost."

Anya kicked a pile of coins and exclaimed, "Thunderbolts! I told you we should have separated them!"

"There's nothing to be done about it now. We have to get back." To Brenwar, he asked, "Will the apparatus work without all five stones?"

"It will work. But will it get the job done?" Brenwar raised his eyebrows. "That's a different matter."

Grey Cloak nodded. "Thank you, Brenwar."

Brenwar grumbled and said, "Do me a favor and tell Nath hello."

"I will." Grey Cloak faced his companions. "It's time to return." Placing his finger on the button of his collar, he said, "All together. One, two, three..."

Each of them pressed their buttons. *Blink.*

DARK MOUNTAIN

From the top of Black Frost's temple, the humongous dragon let out an ear-splitting roar that shook the sky. His guardian dragons, posted on the temple's outer rim, cowered under their wings.

Dirklen lay on the roof in the fetal position with his hands pinned over his ears. He screamed, but his voice was drowned out. He shook so much that his teeth and bones rattled. His innards became like goo. Looking up, he saw Black Frost rise.

The dragon became taller, growing like a mountain bursting from the earth.

Dirklen crawled away on shaking limbs, not stopping until his back was against the safety of the exterior wall.

Black Frost's rage was clear. His maw opened wide, and scorching blue flames shot out. His head dropped, and the flames came with it. He wiped out an entire row of dragons with a single breath.

Grand dragons and middlings took flight with their scales burning to a crisp. In their final act of life, they soared upward, only for their bodies to collapse. With a final screech, they plummeted toward the jagged peaks.

The hot wave of energy from Black Frost's breath scorched the hair on Dirklen's legs and arms like he'd been touched by a hot iron. "Ugh!"

Doubt crept into his mind. He'd been faithful to his master but wasn't sure to what end. Deep in his bowels, he felt and saw Black Frost for what he really was—a monster. But he'd made his choice, and he would have to live with it.

Black Frost lowered. "Come."

Dirklen scrambled to his feet. His steps splashed over the once-icy rooftop. He dropped to both knees and bowed before his master. "What is your wish?"

"I want details. Tell me about this Apparatus of Ruune."

Dirklen spoke of every detail that he recalled.

With an angry sigh, Black Frost said, "These meddlers. These pests. These fools. Once again, they have slipped my grasp. I have been betrayed. My allies have failed me." He tapped one of his talons on the rooftop. "They escaped the Flaming Fence, and I was not told. Watch, Dirklen. Learn. Today you will understand what power truly is."

Dirklen turned as, out of thin air, a circular portal

opened. Flames surrounded a vast underground city. "The Nether Realm," he muttered.

"Yes. It's time I paid an old friend of mine a visit."

The image soared over a broken wasteland of rock, dirt, and dust. It swept through the city streets to a great palace with many stairs. After moving through the hallways, the image came to a stop in a grand library, where a gaunt, long-limbed giant sat behind a desk.

"Utlas!" Black Frost said.

The giant lurched in his chair. "B-Black Frost! To what do I owe the pleasure?"

"Play no games with me! Where are my prisoners, Grey Cloak and Dyphestive?"

Utlas hurried from behind his desk, fell on his hands and knees, and said, "My lord, they have escaped. I have no explanation. I don't know how they did it."

"Lies! Why didn't you tell me they escaped?" The floors, walls, and shelves shook when Black Frost spoke. "Why?"

With his hands clasped together, Utlas said, "I feared for my life. What little is left of it. Call it self-preservation."

Black Frost's eyes narrowed. "If you wish to live, tell me all I need to know, and you will find my favor. What about the Helm of the Dragons? I take it it's still secured?"

Utlas swallowed.

"No," Black Frost said with widening eyes.

Dirklen spotted a glimmer of fear in the dragon.

"Tell me what happened!" Black Frost demanded. "Tell me all!"

"Zanna Paydark stole it," Utlas said. "She deceived—"

"Impossible!" Black Frost's breath turned hot. "She is a statue in my temple. Dirklen, go and see!"

Dirklen ran down the temple steps to the statue chamber. He'd seen it many times before.

Olgstern Stronghair was in place, but Zanna's statue was that of the elf Datris, whom he'd encountered in the past.

He raced back to Black Frost's platform. "She's gone."

Black Frost snarled. "Now I see the deception. Gossamer and Datris slipped it right by my eyes." He turned to Utlas. "For this transgression, you will die!"

Utlas rose and shook his fist at Black Frost. "Do what you will. I have not lived well, but I think I've lived long enough to see you defeated! My final wish is to wish your enemies well!"

"Silence!" The dragon's burning gaze turned Utlas into ashes, then the portal closed. He raised his voice higher. "I tire of this world and its pesky heroes. The time to destroy all hope has come. War is coming, Grey Cloak and Dyphestive. Every living thing will fall in my wake, and you will be at fault! Riskers and Black Guard, you are my wrath. I turn you loose!"

Black Frost's gaze fell upon Dirklen. "Now, I will give you power unlike any man has known before. Use your

Thunderstone. Find them. Slay them all!" He touched Dirklen with the tip of his talon. "But I have placed a curse upon you. Betray me, and you will die."

Power fed from the dragon's talon into Dirklen. He threw his arms back and gasped. Strands of blue lightning danced all over his body armor and pierced him to the bone.

Black Frost withdrew his talon and asked, "How do you feel?"

Steam rose from Dirklen's body. Heart pounding like a hammer on an anvil, he looked Black Frost dead in the eye, sneered, and in his own dark manner, said, "I feel invincible."

"That's because you are. Hunt down Talon." Black Frost spread his great wings. "I'll take care of the towers!"

The final battle begins!

Can Dirklen and Black Frost be defeated?

Are Talon's plans to save the world foiled?

How can the heroes stop them when the enemy knows their plan?

You can't stop now! Grab the next book ...

Thunder Time: Dragons Wars Book 19 on sale now! LINK!

PLEASE, DON'T FORGET TO LEAVE A REVIEW, THANKS!

REVIEW LINK FOR RIDE THE SKY THE SKY BOOK 18!

You can learn more about the strange world of Nalzambor in the Chronicles of Dragon Collection. On Sale Now!

LINK

And if you haven't already, signup for my newsletter and grab 3 FREE books including the Dragon Wars Prequel. WWW.DRAGONWARSBOOKS.COM

Teachers and Students, if you would like to order paperback copies for you library or classroom, email craig@ thedarkslayer.com to receive a special discount.

Gear up in this Dragon Wars body armor enchanted with a +2 Coolness factor/+4 at Gaming Conventions. Sizes range from halfling (Small) to Ogre (XXL). LINK . www.society6.com

ABOUT THE AUTHOR

*Check me out on Bookbub and follow: HalloranOn-BookBub

*I'd love it if you would subscribe to my mailing list: www.craighalloran.com

*On Facebook, you can find me at The Darkslayer Report or Craig Halloran.

*Twitter, Twitter, Twitter. I am there, too: www.twitter.com/CraigHalloran

*And of course, you can always email me at craig@thedarkslayer.com

See my book lists below!

OTHER BOOKS

Craig Halloran resides with his family outside his home-town of Charleston, West Virginia. When he isn't entertaining mankind, he is seeking adventure, working out, or watching sports. To learn more about him, go to www.thedarkslayer.com.

Check out all my great stories...

Free Books
>**The Red Citadel and the Sorcerer's Power**
>The Darkslayer: Brutal Beginnings
>Nath Dragon—Quest for the Thunderstone

The Chronicles of Dragon Series 1 (10-book series)
>The Hero, the Sword and the Dragons (Book 1)

Dragon Bones and Tombstones (Book 2)

Terror at the Temple (Book 3)

Clutch of the Cleric (Book 4)

Hunt for the Hero (Book 5)

Siege at the Settlements (Book 6)

Strife in the Sky (Book 7)

Fight and the Fury (Book 8)

War in the Winds (Book 9)

Finale (Book 10)

Boxset 1-5

Boxset 6-10

Collector's Edition 1-10

Tail of the Dragon, The Chronicles of Dragon, Series 2 (10-book series)

Tail of the Dragon #1

Claws of the Dragon #2

Battle of the Dragon #3

Eyes of the Dragon #4

Flight of the Dragon #5

Trial of the Dragon #6

Judgement of the Dragon #7

Wrath of the Dragon #8

Power of the Dragon #9

Hour of the Dragon #10

Boxset 1-5

Boxset 6-10

Collector's Edition 1-10

The Odyssey of Nath Dragon Series (New Series) (Prequel to Chronicles of Dragon)

Exiled

Enslaved

Deadly

Hunted

Strife

The Darkslayer Series 1 (6-book series)

Wrath of the Royals (Book 1)

Blades in the Night (Book 2)

Underling Revenge (Book 3)

Danger and the Druid (Book 4)

Outrage in the Outlands (Book 5)

Chaos at the Castle (Book 6)

Boxset 1-3

Boxset 4-6

Omnibus 1-6

The Darkslayer: Bish and Bone, Series 2 (10-book series)

Bish and Bone (Book 1)

Black Blood (Book 2)

Red Death (Book 3)

Lethal Liaisons (Book 4)

Torment and Terror (Book 5)

Brigands and Badlands (Book 6)

War in the Wasteland (Book 7)

Slaughter in the Streets (Book 8)

Hunt of the Beast (Book 9)

The Battle for Bone (Book 10)

Boxset 1-5

Boxset 6-10

Bish and Bone Omnibus (Books 1-10)

CLASH OF HEROES: Nath Dragon meets The Dark-slayer mini series

Book 1

Book 2

Book 3

The Henchmen Chronicles

The King's Henchmen

The King's Assassin

The King's Prisoner

The King's Conjurer

The King's Enemies

The King's Spies

The Gamma Earth Cycle

Escape from the Dominion

Flight from the Dominion

Prison of the Dominion

The Supernatural Bounty Hunter Files (10-book series)

Smoke Rising: Book 1

I Smell Smoke: Book 2

Where There's Smoke: Book 3

Smoke on the Water: Book 4

Smoke and Mirrors: Book 5

Up in Smoke: Book 6

Smoke Signals: Book 7

Holy Smoke: Book 8

Smoke Happens: Book 9

Smoke Out: Book 10

Boxset 1-5

Boxset 6-10

Collector's Edition 1-10

Zombie Impact Series

Zombie Day Care: Book 1

Zombie Rehab: Book 2

Zombie Warfare: Book 3

Boxset: Books 1-3

OTHER WORKS & NOVELLAS

The Red Citadel and the Sorcerer's Power